"Laura, Are You Awake?"

"Very," she said, impulsively leaning over to brush his lips. He stopped her with a strong grip on her arms.

"Why not?" she asked tremulously. "Just once."

He relaxed his arms and ran a hand under her chin, bending slowly to brush his lips against hers. It was like lighting dry grass with a careless match. He lifted her into his arms, pressing her against him tightly. Laura greedily took his caresses and his deep kisses. They were making up for the weeks when they hadn't rushed into each other's arms.

"That's why not," he whispered hoarsely. "I want no regrets with you."

ANN COCKCROFT

lived several years on the island of Mallorca and created this story hoping to recapture its exotic and beautiful locale. Ann's husband is novelist Luke Rhinehart, whose support helped her shape her first Romance for Silhouette. Together with their three sons, they live in Canaan, New York.

Dear Reader,

I'd like to take this opportunity to thank all of you who have written in with your comments on Silhouette Romances.

We are always delighted to receive your letters, telling us what you like best about Silhouette, our authors, or indeed, anything else you want to tell us. This is a tremendous help to us as we strive to publish the best contemporary romances possible.

All the romances from Silhouette Books are for you, so enjoy this book and the many stories to come. I hope you will continue to share your thoughts with us and invite you to write to me at this address:

Jane Nicholls
Silhouette Books
PO Box 177
Dunton Green
Sevenoaks
Kent
TN13 2YE

ANN COCKCROFT
Beloved Pirate

Silhouette *Romance*

Published by Silhouette Books

Copyright © 1984 by Ann Cockcroft

Map by Ray Lundgren

First printing 1984

British Library C.I.P.

Cockcroft, Ann
  Beloved pirate.—(Silhouette romance)
  I. Title
  813'.54[F]   PS3553.02/

  ISBN 0 340 36553 6

Printed and bound in Great Britain for
Hodder and Stoughton Paperbacks, a
division of Hodder and Stoughton Ltd.,
Mill Road, Dunton Green, Sevenoaks,
Kent (Editorial Office: 47 Bedford
Square, London, WC1 3DP) by
Richard Clay (The Chaucer Press) Ltd.,
Bungay, Suffolk

Beloved
Pirate

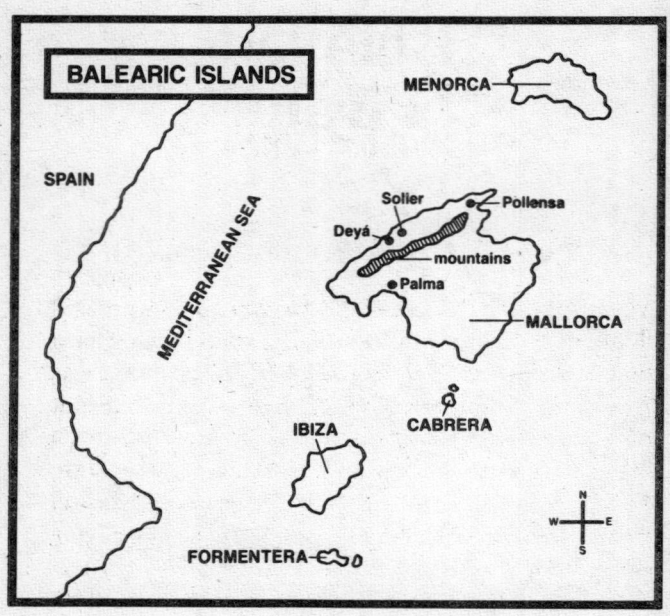

Chapter One

Even after three days on Mallorca, Laura Downes still felt unsettled, transient, as if she were staying in a hotel room for a night rather than in a room that was to be hers for the next eight months. The ancient mountain village of Deyá was too strange, too much like an artist's re-creation for a fairy tale to seem quite real. Though she was surrounded here in the *pensión* by the twenty-five American college students studying at the Creative Arts Institute, it still seemed exotic.

She'd finally finished unpacking, at least. As she sat on the edge of her narrow, hard bed she noted with satisfaction that her room was almost Spartan in its simplicity, with white walls, white tile floors, and only a bureau, a small desk, and a single bookcase holding her books and manuscripts. It was like a nun's cell, she thought, but then smiled as she became aware again of rock music coming from one of the students' rooms down the hall and heard two young women break into excited high-pitched laughter. Her part-time job as "administrative assistant" to Professor Johnson included being a sort of "Mother Superior" to the students, especially the dozen females. None, she was sure, were likely to be as nunlike as the *pensión*'s rooms.

Real or unreal she was here, but she wasn't sure she should be. She missed her family and she missed Bill. Missed him and felt guilty about deciding to spend this year away from him while he finished his internship. They were informally engaged and she knew she had surprised him when she'd accepted Professor Johnson's offer to work part-time and take two writing courses at the Institute. Bill had wanted her to work as a medical secretary at the hospital where he was serving as an intern. It would have meant totally giving up her efforts to write, only half a year after having won the Senior Literary Prize for a play she had written. Worse, it would have meant settling down in her hometown and shelving her own dreams. Now she was here, but for three days she had spent a lot of time trying to pretend she wasn't.

She unflexed her long legs and walked to the single recessed window to gaze out at the cluster of stone houses rising to the peak at the top of the village where the church was. She'd kept herself so busy setting up the Institute library, typing and posting course schedules, and solving students' problems that she hadn't begun to explore the village, the mountain, or the Mediterranean beaches. As she saw her friend Susan Brown and three other students coming down the main street, laughing and flirting with one another, Laura realized she was hiding from her new life behind a forced busyness. She couldn't keep hiding. She and Bill wouldn't be together again until the Christmas holidays; unless she was going to admit she'd made a mistake, she'd better snap out of it.

"You can't go anyplace in this village without hearing the clatter of a typewriter," Susan said, abruptly coming into the room and sitting with a bounce on the bed. "It gives me an inferiority complex." She was a petite blonde, a senior at Darrow College, from which Laura had graduated four months earlier.

"Where'd you go this morning?" Laura asked, turning at the window to smile.

"I interviewed Eric Tabor, the artist," Susan answered, looking around the room, examining the progress Laura had made toward settling in. "At least he doesn't type. I'm supposed to do a series of interviews for the *Long Island Press,* so I figured I'd better start earning my tuition."

"Do you really have a contract?"

"Well, no, but the editor said they'd certainly print any interview I could get with Jared Tanner," Susan replied. "Has he arrived yet?"

"Not that I know of," Laura said, going to her bureau to pick up her brush and absently give her long chestnut hair a few tidying strokes.

"Oh, no," said Susan, her large blue eyes widening. "Don't tell me that the Institute's only big name writer isn't coming?"

"He postponed his flight again," Laura responded, remembering the phone call she'd taken for Professor Johnson the day before in which a brusque voice had announced that something had come up and he still couldn't leave.

"Well, he'd better," Susan said, relaxing. "I'd hate to think I'd wasted my money. Jared Tanner was one of the main reasons I decided to study here. Besides," she added, her eyes sparkling mischievously, "what a hunk."

Laura laughed. "The real reason emerges at last. His good looks wrote his books." She gave Susan a telling glance.

"It helps to be attractive," Susan defended. "As you should know."

"Yes," said Laura, looking in the mirror in front of her. "But it also helps people ignore everything else about you." She set down her brush and went back to her window. "Any more student complaints about the rooms?" she asked Susan, to change the subject.

"But of course," said Susan cheerfully. "No wall-to-wall carpeting, no private phones, no color TV, no private baths, low water pressure, and worst of all, I heard one student complain, 'Everybody speaks Spanish.'" Susan and Laura both laughed.

"I think I'm going to love it," Laura said. "I feel free without all the usual American distractions."

"Well, come on then," Susan said, jumping up. "If you're free enough to stare out the window, you're free enough to come out to the café with me. I'm scheduled to do some research with Elena Marvin, the poet, and that gorgeous blond guy from Colgate."

In her mercurial fashion Susan grabbed Laura by the arm and led her out of the room. Whether Susan was planning to research the poet or the student from Colgate wasn't clear, and Laura smiled at Susan's ambiguity. She thought of taking a notebook along so she could record some of her impressions for Bill but decided that it would appear pretentious.

Outside the *pensión* the bright September sun lit the fuchsia bougainvillea into an explosion of color where it grew riotously over the sheltered patio. Laura, bursting with energy, began taking long strides up the main street until Susan, with her short legs, had trouble keeping up. Laura finally slowed down to marvel at the row upon row of terraced olive trees that marched up the mountainside. After they passed the *estanco,* the small grocery shop with oranges, olives, blood sausages, long encased cheeses, and strings of small red tomatoes all piled or hanging in the window, Susan pointed up at John Martin, the good-looking blond student she had mentioned. He was waving to them from the open café raised above the road, and they climbed the curved stone steps to join him. John had come into Laura's office downstairs in the *pensión* several times since their arrival, ostensibly about cashing checks or course changes, but had each time hung around to chat.

When they reached the cluster of tables on the stone patio, she saw Elena Marvin, a small honey-blond woman, look up with a smile of welcome for Susan. She and Susan sat down and John asked Laura what she'd like to drink. With Elena sipping coffee, and Susan and John ordering beer, Laura decided to celebrate her escape from work with a rum and Coke. When Susan immediately began asking Elena about her life and work, Laura recognized an unofficial interview beginning.

John raised an eyebrow at Laura and grinned. "Maybe I should write poetry too. It's a great attention getter."

Laura smiled. "You're just jealous."

"Not if I've got your attention, I'm not."

"Oh?" Laura leaned back in her chair, crossing her

long jean-clad legs. "Tell me about your life and career then," she added, keeping her tone light.

"It started getting very exciting as of one minute ago."

"You mean your beer is that good!"

John laughed. "It's getting better with each sip." He smiled at her. "I've noticed you've been shackled to your desk up till now and haven't had a chance to see much of the village. There's a churchyard at the top of the hill with a 360 degree view that's worth a hike. Are you free to come with me?"

Laura was saved from having to decide when Professor Johnson appeared on the terrace.

"There you are, Laura," he said, hurrying up to their table. "I've been looking all over for you." Professor Johnson was a big-boned fiftyish man with a square-jowled, pleasant face. In a rumpled brown tweed suit, he seemed harried.

"What's wrong?" Laura asked.

"I just got a telegram," Professor Johnson said. "Jared Tanner is finally arriving. His plane is scheduled to land in about an hour in Palma. I've got an appointment then, so I want you to take a taxi down and meet him."

"Of course," said Laura, standing, but disappointed she had to leave.

"He's three days late," Professor Johnson went on peevishly. "But we can still be accommodating. I worked hard to get him to come to Mallorca to teach. It's a feather in our cap."

"Where can I get a taxi?" Laura asked, aware of Susan smiling and whispering to John.

"It's two blocks below your *pensión*. You'd better hurry or you'll be late. And thanks, Laura."

Laura left the last of her drink, said good-bye to her companions, and walked quickly back to her room to change. She pulled off jeans and a yellow knit shirt and put on a simple white sheath and white sandals. Then she hurried down the hill to find the taxi.

As she rode down the winding road toward Palma, Laura realized that she felt a slight dislike of Jared Tanner without ever having met him. The only book of his she'd read was his short nonfiction tour de force, *The Female of the Species,* a bitterly sardonic jeremiad against women. He implied that most women were scheming spiders who, once they had captured the male's love, devoured him, sapping him of his creative talents and turning him into a respectable and unoriginal breadwinner. Although she'd read someplace that he'd recently disavowed some of the sentiments in the book, his playboy reputation also created in her a sense of distaste.

She hoped she could recognize him at the airport from the glossy black-and-white photograph of the author on the book's cover. As she sat in the back of the cab and thought of the sensuous and arrogant face of that photo, she smiled to herself sardonically: This was the man who was supposed to help her perfect her play- and story-writing? He looked like he wouldn't condescend to notice anyone who hadn't written at least two best-sellers.

The taxi was late arriving at the airport. It had left

Deyá on schedule, but the driver was unhurried and the trip seemed endlessly delayed in Palma's traffic. Laura's effort in Spanish to get the little man at the wheel to drive faster produced nothing but "Si, si," and more dawdling.

As she hurriedly walked into the air terminal and headed toward the flight desk, she braced herself to meet an irate author. Her worst fears were confirmed. The jet had arrived half an hour ago. She knew she would have to search for him; he would not know who was coming to meet him. Her heart raced briefly as she began looking for the face she had seen on the jacket of the novel. When she wanted to ask a porter about Mr. Tanner, not a single Spanish sentence came into her head to begin describing him.

Finally, out of the corner of her eye she saw a tall dark-haired man leaning against the Hertz rental car counter. He was filling out papers. There was something about the profile that drew her forward. A brown suede jacket stretched across broad shoulders, and fawn-colored trousers cleanly fit long muscular legs. The man wore an aura of confidence and strength that was striking.

As she approached she heard his deep masculine voice caressing the Spanish language as he exchanged questions and answers with the pretty, flustered young woman serving him. Laura stood awkwardly waiting for him to finish.

"Mr. Tanner?" she asked finally.

He turned his head slowly toward her at the sound of his name.

"Yes?" he asked quietly, his dark eyes running quickly over her. He managed to make her acutely conscious of the white dress molding her shapely figure and of her bare tanned legs. His eyes gentled, and a brief smile pulled at his firm mouth.

"What can I do for you?" he asked, but immediately he turned away to conclude his business at the counter and pocketed the papers.

Laura fought her annoyance of his frank appraisal of her figure and his equally quick dismissal. She noted his smile to the pretty attendant. He finally turned once more to her, his eyes again registering interest.

She calmly held out her hand to him. "I'm Laura Downes, Professor Johnson's assistant," she said more briskly than was necessary. "I've a taxi waiting outside to take you to Deyá." She nodded in the direction of the sliding doors.

He gave her offered hand a brief warm squeeze and smiled. "Dismiss it," he said. "I've just rented a car. Or did you think I was ordering dinner?"

Laura felt a flash of resentment at his sarcasm. His smile broadened at her loss of composure.

"Of course," she said. "But you can cancel it and take the cab if you'd like."

"No," he replied. "I want the car. Why don't you point out the taxi to me and I'll take care of it." He confidently moved toward the doors of the terminal. She turned to follow him, unable to do anything else. He slowed to take her arm as they went through the automatic doors.

"Is that the one?" he asked.

She nodded. He released her arm and in rapid Spanish took care of the taxi, paying the man generously.

"My car is over there." Jared pointed to a small brown Fiat being loaded with his luggage. "Shall we go?"

"I don't have much choice," she said, walking beside him toward the car. "I was sent to take care of you but our roles seem to have been reversed."

"Johnson didn't have to send anyone," he countered as he bent to open the car door for her. "I'm used to taking care of myself."

"That's obvious, Mr. Tanner."

"It's Jared," he said to her as she seated herself. "And I'm glad you've come. You're much nicer to look at than the Fiat's dashboard."

Laura flushed as he smiled at her and closed the passenger door. He disappeared to go around to the driver's side. His take-charge ways and glibness were confirming her image of him as a conceited playboy. But she shouldn't be rude. Professor Johnson had been quite clear about accommodating his star author. She let out a sigh of resignation as he slid behind the wheel.

"I hope you'll forgive me for changing your plans," he said, and then, seeming to sense her resistance to him, added: "Or are we sworn enemies?"

"There's nothing to forgive," she replied.

"Good," he said, turning on the ignition and putting the car in gear.

As he pulled the car effortlessly into traffic she gave him a sidelong glance. His dark good looks were emphasized by the white open-necked shirt and brown jacket. Thick black hair curled over his collar. When he looked over at her, briefly catching her eyes with his, she felt oddly as if she had been touched by him.

"I'll have to thank Mr. Johnson for sending you. He mentioned he had a secretary. It hadn't occurred to me she would be young and beautiful."

He's flattering me, Laura thought, recognizing the light tone. She had been expecting something like it but had hoped she might be wrong. She sat straighter in the seat.

"I hope you had a nice flight," she said redirecting the conversation.

"I slept," he said.

"The entire flight?"

"Almost. I think I ate something once or twice but fortunately don't remember anything about it. I cut short one of my appointments in New York and rushed to make the plane. I'm glad now I did." He was grinning at her. She was surprised to find how much his smile transformed his strong serious face into a warm friendly one. She was disturbingly aware of his power to charm.

"Your first trip abroad?" he asked casually as he headed the car up the mountain.

"How did you know?" she asked.

"Just a guess."

A small knot appeared between her winged eyebrows.

"Don't frown," he said. "Youth is a valuable asset, particularly for a woman. You don't want to have wrinkles before your time unless they're the creases of smiles. I think you've got a lot to smile about."

Another male prelude, she thought, and didn't answer.

"Am I disturbing you?" he asked.

"No," she answered quickly.

"Liar."

"You're outrageous, Mr. Tanner, as I'm sure you know."

He laughed, his brown eyes lighting with play. "Is it my direct approach that bothers you?" He paused and then added, "And please call me Jared." Laura could feel his eyes on her.

She rolled the car window completely down and let the wind blow her long hair around. It released some of the tension building in her.

"I'm not disturbed. . . ." she finally said.

He didn't respond right away. Instead he concentrated on his driving and then changed the subject.

"How long have you been working for Mr. Johnson?" he asked.

"He likes to be called Professor Johnson," Laura said.

"I'll remember that."

"Essentially I've just started my job. It's only part-time," Laura said. "I get to take two courses and my expenses are paid."

"Is mine one of them?" he asked.

"Yes."

"Have you written much?"

"Some." Laura crossed her legs and looked over at him. He was checking a road sign and gearing down. They had begun the long winding climb to Deyá.

"I'll look forward to reading something you've written."

"I'd like that. Thank you."

"So formal." He smiled. "Do I still make you uneasy?"

"I'm just wary," Laura admitted slowly. "I've heard a lot about you . . . and I'm engaged," she said defensively. She saw him quickly scan her ringless fingers.

She wished she hadn't admitted her wariness.

"Engaged?" Jared echoed easily. "And is the lucky man here?"

"No. He's an intern on Long Island." She stiffened. She was not about to go into the details of her private life. Jared glanced at her.

"Sounds like it may be a long engagement."

"It has to be," she replied sharply. "From what I hear you seem to prefer something shorter."

Jared's brows raised briefly and he threw back his head and laughed.

"And exactly what have you heard?" They had slowed to pass through the beautiful village of Valledemosa.

Laura shifted uncomfortably a moment. "I read your book, *The Female of the Species*. You implied that women were best taken in short doses. Being a woman, I took exception." She congratulated herself secretly for not alluding to the rumors in the scandal magazines.

"Oh that," he said, smiling. "I've often wished I'd never let that book escape my pen. You're not the first nor, I'm afraid, the last to complain. Believe me, I don't think all women are witches."

She glanced over at him. "I'm glad to hear it," she said.

"Only most of them," he countered, grinning, and they both laughed. "I wrote that book in three weeks. It hit the market at a time when the Women's Liberation movement was the hottest topic in town. My publisher's eyes lit up with double figures. I was paid well then, and since publication *I've* paid."

Laura laughed at his exasperated tone.

He cocked an eyebrow at her. "I'm glad you're enjoying my suffering."

"It makes you human."

"And I thought I was born human." He laughed. "I wonder how many women see men as beasts preying on them?" He paused. "Do you, Laura?"

"Sometimes, yes."

"Now?" he asked.

Laura leaned her head against the seat. "No. You're a guest of the Institute and will be my teacher. I don't think beyond that."

"Will you have dinner with me tonight?"

Laura turned surprised eyes on him. Was this the way he acted with all women, she wondered. "I can't," she said.

"Why not?"

He wasn't going to make it easy for her to refuse. But he disturbed her and she had the feeling he wanted to. She searched for the right diplomatic phrases.

"You're very kind and I thank you for the offer, but I'm expected back at the *pensión*." She reached up to smooth her ruffled hair with both hands.

He gave her a knowing look. He knew she was wiggling out of it without a real excuse. Laura flushed.

"Afraid of me?" A corner of his mouth was curled in amusement.

"Yes." It was his turn to be surprised.

"It passes, you know," he offered quietly. "The best way I know to conquer fear is to face it."

Laura gave an audible sigh of relief as they wound their way into the village. She gave him instructions to get to the *pensión* and told him where he could locate Professor Johnson.

He pulled up outside the *pensión,* and as Laura began to leave he reached for her wrist and held it. She tried to pull free, her eyes locking with his a moment.

"Thank you for coming down to meet me, Laura."

"You're welcome. It was part of my job," she replied, immediately regretting the rudeness.

"I had hoped it was something you had wanted to do." He smiled lazily at her and let her go.

Laura felt self-conscious as she walked past the car—as if a pair of dark eyes were sweeping over her, invading her privacy, assessing her womanhood.

Chapter Two

During the following days Laura began to wonder why a writer as successful as Jared Tanner would bother to take this teaching job in a remote mountain village in Spain. From the gossip about him that had been spurred by his arrival, it appeared that for the two years since the publication of *The Female of the Species* he had led a conspicuously public life, appearing on television talk shows, being written about in gossip columns, *People, The National Enquirer*. Why was he now here?

But though she had been struck by Jared's masculine power, she was determined that she would show no sign of the effect he'd had on her. When students gathered around him at the café or after his classes, she made a point of walking away. When Susan wanted to drag her out to walk to the beach because Jared and some others were going, she declined.

Instead she concentrated on settling into the routine of her work and classes and writing newsy letters to Bill. She went to her two writing workshops in the morning, and in the afternoon she often did typing and filing in a small office next to Professor Johnson's.

Occasionally she had to run errands, posting letters, picking up office supplies, or helping some student settle in.

Jared's workshop took most of her free time. He had insisted on their beginning new work using their present experience. They could submit one completed piece to him, although he warned he might not get to read them all right away. When Laura laid her most recent short story on his desk, she suppressed both her hopes and her anxieties. Someone else had submitted what looked like half a novel. His warning seemed justified.

She invariably sat in the back of the classroom, wanting to keep at a distance the effect he sometimes had on her. Watching his dark figure in front of the class, his lazy assurance, she couldn't help but admire the attention he commanded.

"Writing is work and demands self-discipline," he said to them during their third meeting. "If you don't like that aspect of it, there's no point in beginning. I expect nothing from you; it's what you expect of yourselves that will make the difference." He sat on the edge of a heavy wooden table that served as a desk. "I want to read about what you feel, not what you think you should feel or what you think I want to read."

Laura glanced over at a student named Sheila who was enraptured. Laura made a face to herself, looking up briefly to see Jared's eyes finding hers.

"Any questions, Miss Downes?" A touch of humor edged his voice.

Daunted by his catching her look at Sheila, Laura shook her head. Others did have questions relating to what they had been writing. He answered them briefly, urging them to find and use their own voices, concluding with, "Write about real experiences, real feelings."

Laura frowned. She wasn't sure that she wanted to write about her real feelings. But what was she going to write about, more descriptions of Deyá? Her reactions to the people who lived on the island? She missed some of his talk, but then heard him say: "Miss Downes, I'd like to see you after class."

She waited at the back of the room until the usual cluster of students around his desk had finally gone or been dismissed. When she and Jared were finally alone, she walked slowly to the front of the room. Jared drew on the tan corduroy jacket he had slung on a chair, quite coolly letting the time pass. Laura felt her nerves go taut. He stood casually watching her as he adjusted the back of his collar. She turned her face upward to look at him directly. Brown eyes met green ones and she flushed, making her angry at both herself and him. Bill never looked at her this way.

"You make me nervous," she said in a rush.

"Why?" he asked, moving to stand near her.

"I don't know," she said in a low voice.

"Can you write about it?" he asked quietly.

"What is there to write about?"

"Your own feelings."

"I doubt it."

"Are they real, your feelings?"

"Real?" She raised her eyes to his uncertainly.

"Yes, real, not fiction, some schoolgirl fantasy."

"You're imagining things, Mr. Tanner. I'm not a

schoolgirl and I have no schoolgirl fantasies, none at all, and nothing I'd want to write about."

He smiled, a flash of white teeth in his sensuous mouth, his brown eyes amused. "Then you should have no problems."

"None," she said, a hand coming up to toss her long hair back. Her eyes sparked. "You asked to see me?"

"And now I've seen you," he replied, watching her with what seemed a taunting smile.

"I think you're presumptuous, Mr. Tanner," she said, picking up her books again to leave.

He laughed. "Not the stuff fantasies are made of?"

"More like a nightmare!" She started toward the door but stopped. "I'm sorry. I didn't mean to be so . . . impolite." She made a helpless gesture with a hand, nonplussed to find herself trapped in a tangle of unexplained feelings and words.

He came up and put a hand on her bare arm, his eyes serious a moment, his lips parted as if he were about to say something and then closed tightly. Laura felt momentarily stunned; her heart skipped a beat.

"Write about it," he said, smiling wickedly, and releasing her, stepped away into the street.

When she was alone, Laura shivered involuntarily. She felt a physical attraction for him much stronger than anything she had felt before, but she sensed he was purposefully playing with her in a light way and that made her angry. He was probably doing the same with half the women in his classes. She had no respect for that kind of man. She felt a sudden irrational annoyance with Bill for not preventing her from coming to Mallorca. She didn't think Jared was the

sort of man who would let his intended fly off some-
where for a long separation.

She continued to work hard both for Professor
Johnson and for her two courses, not wanting to let
down herself or her instructors, even Jared. She might
be determined to be indifferent to him as a man, but
her pride in her writing made her want to please him
as a teacher.

Five days later Professor Johnson asked her to
find Jared. A Palma television crew was driving up
to the village in two hours to tape an interview with
him that would make excellent publicity for the Institute.

"The students say he went down to the *cala*,"
Professor Johnson said. "Go down and see if you can
find him and ask him to be up here at the *pensión* by
four o'clock."

Laura agreed, deciding that since she had to go to
the beach, she might as well take advantage of it and
go for a swim. After Professor Johnson left, she
changed into her swimsuit, pulled on jeans and a knit
shirt, stuffed a towel and a comb into her *thesta,* and
hurried off.

The hike down the winding, rocky mountain road
to the *cala* provided spectacular views of the coastline
and sea. The air was crystal, the water an unbeliev-
able shade of turquoise graduating into deep purple.
Pine forests and terraced olive groves spilled down
toward the water along the coast, and five hundred
feet below her the tiny human figures on the beach
appeared like insects.

When she finally emerged through a narrow ravine
into the hundred-yard-wide cove that cupped the local

beach, she saw that about half of the twenty or so people present were from the Institute. Susan and John waved at her as she searched for Jared. When she finally saw him, she felt an odd contraction in her chest: He was sitting against a rock with Elena Marvin. Both were in bathing suits and Laura was struck by Jared's tanned, well-muscled body. Elena's daring one-piece blue suit revealed a lot of cleavage. They looked like they were enjoying themselves.

"I've got a message from Professor Johnson," Laura announced to Jared, stopping a few feet in front of him.

Jared looked up at her with a smile.

"What is it?" he asked.

"He says a Palma television crew is coming up to interview you at four," Laura replied. "He wants you to be in the *pensión* then."

Jared looked away and stopped smiling.

"I can't make it," he said abruptly.

"You can't?" she said, surprised.

"No, I can't make it," he repeated, looking coldly past her out to sea.

"Professor Johnson said the Institute could use the publicity," Laura persisted.

"Fine. Have them interview him," said Jared.

"What should I tell him then?"

"That I can't make it." Jared's lips and jaw were rigid. He seemed like a different person.

"Why not, Jared?" Elena asked. "It might be fun to see you appear on TV between the bullfights and the *fútbol*."

"I'm sorry, Laura," Jared said. "I'm not giving any interviews on Mallorca." He moved past her and in a half dozen long strides had plunged neatly into the sea.

Elena watched him, shrugged, and began to take off her sunglasses to join him. Laura left to go to the little café built into one corner of the cliff to telephone Professor Johnson about Jared's decision.

When she came back down onto the beach ten minutes later, she was feeling depressed and felt like leaving. Professor Johnson had been annoyed with her for Jared's intransigence, implying she hadn't been very persuasive. But John Martin captured her before she could escape and led her down to where he and Susan had spread out their towels. As Laura lowered her *thesta* she saw Susan peering over at Jared and Elena, who were again sunbathing against the rock.

"I wonder if Elena is the next on Jared's list," Susan speculated, eyeing them unashamedly as Laura spread out her towel on the somewhat stony stretch of beach. "Imagine the poetry that would come out of that."

Laura laughed. "Susan," she said as she slowly peeled off her jeans and red T-shirt to reveal her black bikini. "One of these days someone is going to overhear your remarks and repeat them, and you're going to have to answer for them." She noticed John's frank admiration of her curves as she adjusted herself on her towel.

"I'm always quite careful about my more audacious comments," said Susan, smiling. "But come on, do you think they are? Lovers, I mean."

Laura rolled over on her stomach, avoiding looking in the direction of Jared and Elena thirty feet away.

"I don't know and don't care and neither should you. They're both adults and free to do as they choose."

Susan unbuckled her pink bikini top to get sun on her back, snuggling her small figure down in her towel.

"I hope they're not," she said. "Elena's so obvious. Look at the way she smiles at Jared. She only comes down here when he's around."

"Meow!" said John, teasing her. "Wasn't that your poem she read to the class this morning, saying something about journalists having no poetry in their souls, and that's why they're journalists?"

"Ouch!" Susan said.

"Let's go for a swim," Laura suggested, getting up and not wanting the discussion to continue.

"We just went," said Susan.

Laura took off her sunglasses, unflexed her long slender body, and moved gracefully into the water. Having grown up by the seashore on Long Island she was in her natural element. She dived in, not caring if anyone followed, and swam far out toward a rocky ledge protruding from the sheer cliff face forty yards away. After climbing out she lay on her stomach with eyes closed to sun herself in peace. After a few moments she heard someone approach, and her heart gave an unexpected flutter. But it was John, and an odd feeling of deflation crept through her.

"You swim like a fish," he said as he hauled himself out to join her. "Where'd you learn?"

"I grew up on a beach," Laura explained.

"More likely on a houseboat where you had to

swim back and forth every day." John laughed as he stretched out beside her. Gently he put his arm across her back. When he felt her tension he removed it.

"Sorry," he said, "but you look so beautiful in that suit."

Laura sat up, not certain what to say in response.

"Thank you," she replied simply.

John turned on his side, raising himself up on an elbow.

"I have the impression you want to keep me at a distance. Is that right?" he asked without rancor.

"I like you, John," she replied easily, "but . . . I'm engaged." She felt a little hypocritical and wanted to reach out a hand to touch his arm resting near hers but thought better of it.

"Ah, that's the reason," said John with a smile. "It seems like a strange engagement to me—him back in the States and you here . . ."

"He's an intern at Brookhaven Hospital and has to live there for a year," Laura defended her absent fiancé.

"Is there a date set for the wedding?"

"Not yet," she replied, putting up both hands and nervously smoothing her long wet hair.

"So at least I can take your mind off your separation?" John suggested, smiling.

"Oh, yes, you can do that," Laura said, smiling back.

"I'm not asking for the moon, just a little sunshine, a little fun. Is that allowed?"

"Of course. Bill and I don't expect each other to enter a cloister. We agreed we'd both enjoy ourselves . . ." Laura wondered why her words sounded strange to her ears. It hadn't seemed wrong when she and Bill had discussed the "terms" of their separation a few weeks before. Bill hadn't seemed bothered at all by her possibly going out with other men. She irritably wondered whether he thought no one would ask her.

John sat up. "Have you heard about the hike up the mountain next week? The art teacher is organizing it. Will you come?"

"I'd love to," Laura answered. "I'd like nothing better than to hike around this island." She stood up beside him. "Race you to shore," she added and, with a surge, dived in.

John quickly followed her. He was a good swimmer, but she was better and held her lead all the way to the beach. As she emerged from the water beside John she was suddenly aware of Jared less than ten yards away staring at her. Walking back to where Susan waited on the beach, she felt as if she were parading nude on a burlesque stage. Even back on her towel she didn't relax until he and Elena rose and left.

At the end of her second week of classes, Laura turned in her first new paper to Jared. She felt it was a good, vivid description of both the village and its people, full of her reactions to being in a foreign culture. She had also written about her personal feelings in a long journal-like series of pages but then shelved them.

She felt she deserved a break and that Saturday took a long walk below the village along a path that wound above the Mediterranean. The sea stretched blue below her, pine trees were singing in the wind, and jagged cliffs fell precipitously down into the clear depths of the water. She was happy to be alone for once, without Susan chattering beside her, or John, who, of late, was pressing her into a more than friendly relationship. That night there was to be an open-house party. The students and faculty had invited the community in for a get-together, breaking the social ice and hoping to increase contacts between the school and the local community. But today was hers and she felt free and loose and the island was beautiful.

Walking over to the edge of the cliff, she saw a narrow path leading to a place where she could scramble down to the water. She couldn't resist. Following it down, she discovered a ledge and a circle of rocks around a deep tidal pool. It was so clear she could see the brown sea urchins clinging to the bottom. The rocky shore undulating along the coast concealed a hundred small coves hiding similar treasures. She was glad she had worn her swimsuit.

Shedding her jeans and cotton shirt, she sought a good footing and then dived in. As she surfaced she gave an audible sigh of contentment. She explored the bottom of the pool, careful not to touch the needle-sharp brown sea urchins, splashing around until she began to get gooseflesh.

Getting out of the pool, however, was not so simple. As she searched for a ledge under the water to haul herself out, she wished she had given some thought to the problem before so blithely diving in.

Finally, she found what she thought was a good stepping rock. As she scrambled out she gave a piercing scream of pain. She had stepped on an urchin and then scraped her knees.

Trembling, she sat on the dry ledge examining her foot, fighting the pain. She saw several sharp black needles jutting from her heel.

As she was making an effort to extract them, finding it difficult, a man's figure appeared suddenly over a rock on the other side of the pool. Laura's head shot up and she looked straight into Jared's eyes.

"What's the trouble?" he asked. Seeing the blood on her scraped knees, he set a fishing rod down and jumped around the rocks toward her.

Laura turned for her clothes, but they weren't within reach. Jared, seeing her embarrassment, brought them over to her.

"Where did you come from?" she asked, pulling on the blouse he handed her.

He ignored the question. "Are you hurt badly?" His eyes roved over her, finally fixing on the black needles.

"I stepped on a sea urchin, but I think I can manage," she said as he sat down and reached for her foot.

He looked up at her. "You'd better get those spines out. They can cause a severe infection."

"I've been trying to," she snapped.

He gently lifted her foot onto his leg.

"What are you doing here?" she asked.

"I was fishing," he said disinterestedly, examining her foot. "You're lucky. There are only four, and they haven't gone in deep." He reached into his pants pocket, taking out a knife.

"Now what?" Laura asked, eyeing the tool he had in his hand.

"Try to relax. I'm going to take out those spines."

"That's what I was afraid of," she murmured tensely.

"Hold still." He yanked at a spiny needle and Laura gave a groan.

"Once more," he said firmly.

She grimaced as he pulled the last one out.

He gently released her foot and began dabbing with his handkerchief at her right knee, which was covered with blood.

"No Band-aids, I'm afraid," he said, "but I'll wrap my handkerchief around it." Deftly he bent to wet an edge of the towel to clean her scrapes, his black head tilted in concentration. "There," he said, smiling at her when he'd finished. "And you're still alive, right?"

She smiled gratefully.

"Still alive. Thank you."

Laura was suddenly aware that Jared's hand was still on her bare leg and that he was looking at her with a knowing smile.

"Traditionally the knight receives . . . a more tangible reward," he suggested softly, making Laura acutely conscious of her seminakedness and of the way his glowing eyes had lowered to her lips.

"If you'll excuse me," she said hurriedly, standing up, "I'd like to put on my jeans."

"What a shame," Jared said, still smiling. "Are you

sure you wouldn't like to get out of your wet suit first? A part of the towel is still usable."

"No, thanks," Laura replied, giving him a quelling look. She reached for her jeans and began to put them on.

"Here," he said, picking up the towel and flipping it to her. "At least dry your hair with it."

She caught the towel and for the moment put it around her neck. As she finished putting on her jeans Jared turned away and gathered up his fishing rod.

"I think I'll continue my fishing awhile," he said quietly, his back to her. "If you care to stay I'd enjoy your company." She wasn't certain of his mood, but when he turned and gave her a serious look his dark eyes sent surprising warmth through her. Without waiting for an answer he climbed down the rocks with his pole to the edge of the sea.

Laura watched as he cast a line out and stood patiently reeling it in. She knew she ought to leave, yet remained, watching him. She scrubbed her long hair with the towel until it was almost dry.

"I would never have thought you liked fishing," she said spontaneously to his back.

"Why not?" he threw over his shoulder.

"I don't know. My impression of you has been that you were too sophisticated for such a simple pleasure."

"I find it relaxing," he answered. "I'm getting tired of the sophisticated life."

"Have you ever taught before?" she asked, wanting to know more about him.

"No, this is the first time."

Laura stretched out on a rock, feeling the sun's soothing rays and beginning to relax from the earlier tension.

"Why did you take this job?" she continued.

He reeled in his line slowly, not answering at first.

"You don't have to answer if you'd rather not," she added.

"I don't mind telling you," he said as he sat down on a rock to adjust his reel. He still wasn't looking at her. "The hustle of the literary world was getting to me. The publicity generated by that impulsive book I wrote on women had made my life too hectic with promotion, controversy, and attention. I felt I was beginning to lose a sense of who I really am. I need some time to be by myself again and reevaluate what I'm doing." He paused briefly, now staring down into the water lapping the rocks near his feet. "But the world seems to be catching up with me even here."

Laura wasn't certain what he meant by the last remark but decided against asking.

"Perhaps you bring your world with you," she suggested quietly.

"Yes," he said, a trace of anger in his voice. He put his pole down and turned to face her, the wind ruffling his thick black hair. "Any more questions?" he asked, an eyebrow raised.

Laura put her arms behind her head.

"Oh, I can think of a few." She flashed him a smile.

"Are you sure you're not a reporter for the *Long Island Press* too?" he asked, a trace of smile on his face.

"Positive."

Jared's face slowly clouded.

"Unfortunately, I'm afraid I can't trust you," he said.

"Most people are honest if given a chance," she said.

"No, they're not. Everyone wears a mask, especially around someone they think is famous. Lately I've learned to distrust everyone."

"I don't wear a mask," Laura countered.

"It's thin," he corrected her, "but you wear one. My guess is it's a cover for your feelings, which you're afraid to reveal. Even to yourself."

As she looked at him uncertainly she wasn't able to hold his gaze. "I don't think I'll pursue that one," she finally said.

"I didn't think you would," he replied casually.

"Have you ever been married?" Laura asked, thinking of his *Female of the Species* book. She adjusted her position, raising her head up against the rock behind her. When he looked up and studied her a moment something grabbed her in the pit of her stomach and made her regret her running tongue.

"I'm sorry," she managed in a low voice. "That was tactless of me."

"The answer is no." He held his head very steady, his eyes half-closed as they fixed on her face.

"But you've had plenty of experience."

He was very still. Then he stood and climbed up the rocks to stand in front of her. He reached out a hand to catch her chin firmly, raising it up. "Where are you going with this conversation, Laura, do you know?"

"I didn't mean to say that," she said, embarrassed. When she reached up to disengage his hand, their mingled touch sent a sensual shock through her. He withdrew his hand and stared down at her. The sea sloshed in and out of the tidal pool, the slap of water against the cliffs the only sound. As their eyes met and fused and then his eyes dropped again to her lips, Laura felt suddenly weak.

"I'm sorry for my . . ." she began to whisper, aware of both her powerful attraction to him and her distrust. When she instinctively placed a hand on his chest, she saw a light leap in his eyes. Then she felt his mouth on hers, warm and firm.

As he lowered himself beside her his hand tangled in her hair and he pressed her close. She unthinkingly brought her arms up around him and felt his kiss become more demanding, probing her response. She felt an ecstatic desire to receive and return his kiss, a captive of the unexpected pleasure she felt. When he released her mouth to press his lips against the sensitive curve of her neck she groaned and arched her back to receive him, letting her own lips trail along his face. But as she felt his hand cupping her breast she was abruptly frightened at her response. She brought her arms around to push back against his chest to try to break away.

As he still held her, his face now a foot away, his dark eyes searched hers as if questioning her sudden change. She could feel the rise and fall of his breathing warm on her face.

"Please, no more," she said huskily, beginning to recover her sense of herself and remembering his reputation.

"No more?" he asked, watching her with glittering eyes. "I thought we were just beginning."

"I'd like to go," she said, trying to pull herself free.

"Go?" he said, a look of annoyance crossing his forehead. "But if this isn't what you expected, why did you follow me down here?"

"Follow you!?" Laura exclaimed, freeing herself at last and standing up.

"Yes, follow me," he said, eyeing her with a frown. "In the last week my female students seem to have accidentally stumbled upon me no matter where I go," he added, now leaning back against a rock. "The only place I'm safe is in the men's room."

Laura swayed with a rush of anger.

"Such arrogance!" she snapped at him fiercely. "I did *not* follow you down here. I did not invite your kiss and I don't have the slightest interest in you."

Jared leaned toward her, a taunting smile appearing on his face.

"Well, maybe a *little* interest," he suggested.

Laura felt her cheeks redden at the allusion to her passionate response to his kisses.

"It's exactly because I *didn't* follow you here and didn't expect what just happened that you caught me by surprise," she said firmly, trying to suppress her anger and embarrassment.

As Jared continued to stare at her his mocking smile dissolved and was replaced by a look of doubt and concern. He slowly rose to his feet.

"Then I'm sorry," he said as she began to limp past him up the hill. He placed his hand on her arm to stop and steady her. "Please, I mean it. I made a mistake. You didn't follow me and it was rude and arrogant of me to assume you had."

As their eyes met Laura found herself trying to decide between anger and distrust on the one hand

and the warmth of his eyes on the other. Then a sudden determination to resist his seductiveness flared. Her cheeks blazed as she remembered again her response to his kisses.

"Rude and arrogant: At least your apology is accurate," she said. "And I accept it." She broke away from him. "Now we can forget about the whole thing." She began clambering cautiously over the rocks to the trail.

"I don't think so, Laura," he said softly to her retreating back.

And as she continued hobbling up the trail toward the village Laura wasn't certain she could forget it so easily either.

Chapter Three

Two hours later Susan discovered Laura brushing her long thick hair after an early supper. Laura had freshly doctored her knees and foot and they felt better. She felt unaccountably vibrant and wanted to dance tonight at the party. Besides, Professor Johnson had practically ordered her to "mingle" with the guests. Susan too was filled with excitement.

"I've been planning and working all day on this get-together and I'm done in. I'm heading for a shower to look my beauteous best." Susan plunked herself down on Laura's bed.

"You look terrific already," Laura said.

"What's with you?" Susan asked, eyeing Laura with her usual keen perception. "You look like the cat that's just caught the mouse."

"Hardly!" Laura exclaimed, discomfitted by Susan's sharp observation. "I just had a lovely swim down in a little tidal pool." She quickly went on to tell her about her walk, the swim, and the sea urchin, but nothing about meeting Jared. She was too uncertain about what had happened with him to begin to try to talk about it.

"You're sure that sea urchin didn't shoot some sort of exotic elixir into you?" Susan persisted, smiling.

"No." Laura laughed.

"Well," said Susan, inspecting her pink nails for imperfections, "you going with anyone tonight?"

"No, of course not. Are you?"

"I thought John might have asked you," Susan suggested. "He's a lot of man, that one, if you go for the blond beach-boy type." She paused, watching Laura. "I wouldn't mind a fling with him," she concluded.

"Welcome," said Laura. "We're only friends. I don't believe in putting a personal label on anyone. And you're forgetting Bill."

"Oh, come off it." Susan giggled. "You don't imagine Bill is sitting home all the time twiddling his stethoscope, do you? When a woman likes a man, she usually hangs a sign on him one way or another saying 'hands off.'"

Laura looked at her reflection in the mirror. She saw that her lips had a too-full look about them, a reminder of Jared's assault on them. A faint flush crossed her cheeks as she remembered.

"What?" she said. "Oh. I don't own Bill, Susan. Or John, or anyone else. That's not my style."

"You think you're above jealousy?" Susan said, bouncing once on the bed. "Do *you* have a lot to learn!" She got up to go. "Wait and see, don't take my word for it: The monster lurks in all of us. Wear that green silk blouse tonight. You look great in it."

"Green, I suppose, being the color I'll eventually turn. Off with you, you're impertinent!"

"Don't I know it," said Susan gaily. "But lovable!" Laughing, she retreated from the room.

"Barely!" agreed Laura, smiling.

She put her brush down. Her hair was at its shining best, a thick chestnut mane down her back. She looked over her clothes thoughtfully. Susan may not have much of an eye for her own coloring, but she did see others. She pulled the green blouse on, deciding that Susan had given her the right advice. It brought out the green in her eyes and the reddish highlights in her hair. A long dark-green and blue print skirt molded itself around her hips as she adjusted the wraparound ties. Her foot still ached, but she ignored it. She finished by adding long jade earrings Bill had given her on her birthday. She stood back to survey the effect in the mirror. She looked wonderful. She only hoped she could act nonchalant when she saw Jared. That he had popped into her mind startled her. What was she thinking of?

When she arrived at the party, most of the students were busily greeting guests, passing sangria and taking turns manning the record player. They had been asked beforehand not to play what Professor Johnson had called the "undanceables," and to keep it soft in tone. The pop tunes of Hall and Oates wafted around the room.

It was crowded, but she could still pick out the tall, dark-clad figure of Jared standing against a wall, surrounded by faculty and visitors. But then she gasped when she saw leaning on his arm not Elena Marvin but one of the most stunning blondes Laura had ever seen, dressed in a pencil-slim blue gown,

simple and elegant, as elegant as her perfectly coiffed
pale blond hair, just touching her bare, tanned shoulders. She was smiling up at Jared, a glass of sangria
held in a long manicured hand. Laura felt an almost
palpable ache and then tried to shrug it off. What was
he to her, after all?

John appeared beside her with two glasses of
sangria.

"You look as if you need this," he said.

"I do," she answered softly.

"You look great, Green Eyes," he said, touching
her hair lightly with his free hand.

Laura managed a smile. She could have almost
hugged him in her relief at his regard of her feelings.
She took his offered arm. "So do you," she murmured
as she took in his navy jacket and tan slacks. He had
even put on a tie for the occasion.

John took her over to a small group of students who
were talking to the artist Eric Tabor, who was puffing
on a cigarette and obviously enjoying himself as he
regaled them with his problems as an artist in this
remote village on Mallorca. Beside him was his wife,
Maria, a round Spanish woman with a sweet face. She
was listening to her husband's comments, occasionally
making her own wry observations.

"I've told my son," Eric Tabor was saying, "to take
up accounting, nothing so ridiculous as art. Only fools
try to get their bread and butter by gouging wood and
rubbing color on pieces of paper." He laughed at his
own description of his life. Several students demured,
praising his work.

Laura was introduced and found herself immediately liking the thin, energetic man. Maria was a Spanish instructor at the school. Both possessed a warmth and sparkle that reached out to those around them.

"Well, what do you think of Deyá?" Eric asked Laura. It was a question that was to be repeated many times. The villagers, native and foreign, were justly proud of their quiet, beautiful world. They liked to hear it praised.

"How could anyone not love it," Laura said, finding herself relaxing in his company and giving him a brief impression of the village and its people as she'd already done in her paper for Jared's class. "It's magical," she said, smiling at him. "We'll never be the same, any of us."

"You don't find it crazy, all these artists running around literally scratching out a living?" He laughed at his own pun.

"You just might turn us all into artists with your enthusiasm," she answered him.

"God protect you, then," he said, laughing, and then was taken away by his wife to meet someone new.

John was pushing her toward the line forming near Jared and his ravishing guest.

"She's famous," she heard John whisper in her ear. "A cover model from New York by the name of May Donnelly. I've seen her in television commercials. She just flew in today."

Laura felt a rush of anger when she heard this. Jared must have known that May was coming even as he embraced her down by the sea. He *had* just been playing with her as with the other students. Her eyes sparkled with annoyance when she realized that he and May made a strikingly handsome couple. Jared was magnificent in his trim black suit, champagne silk shirt, and dark tie. He was totally at ease, introducing May Donnelly to everyone as they filed by. Several men hovered around May. Laura maintained a frozen smile as her turn came, ignoring Jared altogether. Miss Donnelly didn't shake hands. One hand rested lightly on Jared's arm; the other held a glass of wine. She greeted each person with a carefully controlled smile, her high soprano liltingly saying the same phrases, as if she were royalty.

"Hello, how are you. So glad to meet you," Laura heard her say.

"Laura is Professor Johnson's assistant," Jared pointed out in his low voice to May. "And also a student in my workshop." Laura said hello in the quietest of voices. She heard herself repeating the social phrase "I hope you enjoy your stay here." She hoped to walk by quickly, but John remained a few minutes in conversation with the beautiful model. She could feel Jared's eyes on her, but she refused to look directly at him, not wanting to give him the pleasure of seeing her anger.

One of the retired European residents, a Dr. Braun, took her hand and held it too long, moving his plump fingers over the back of hers and trying to engage her in a conversation. Mrs. Braun gave Laura an icy stare and she hastily extracted her hand.

Laura's nerves were strained. It was a relief when the music was turned up and the dancing began. John swept her to the dance floor and she gave herself over to the mindless rhythm, ignoring the pulsing of her injured foot. John was not graceful, but he knew what he was doing and Laura loved to dance. She heard Eric Tabor saying good-byes, claiming these new dances were for the young. But he gaily gave his wife a playful turn until she laughed and said they would be sprawled on the floor in another minute.

Laura danced with other men on the crowded floor and answered their banter unthinkingly. When the music became slower, she found herself back in John's arms. They passed close to Jared and May Donnelly, who, as May's gown permitted only small steps, were dancing in one place.

"Shall we switch partners for this one?" Jared asked John. It was more a statement than a question. He handed May to John.

Laura stiffened as Jared took her lightly into his arms and began leading her to a soft Latin rhythm. Even as she tried to resist him he moved her effortlessly around the floor. He bent his dark head to hers.

"Enjoying yourself?" he asked.

"Yes," she replied coolly.

"Why won't you look at me? Is it because of this morning, or May?" His voice was seductively low.

She took in a breath and looked up at him coldly. "Both," she said. "I don't like feeling I was . . . an afternoon snack."

Jared unexpectedly laughed. "A nibble perhaps . . . hardly a snack."

"In any case I hope I gave you indigestion."

He bent his head to her ear, moving his hand on her back in a caress.

"I'm afraid not," he whispered.

She was angry at his words and even angrier because his hand on her back and his mouth at her ear were stirring her.

"So I notice," she said, her eyes flashing. She broke free from him at the edge of the dance floor. "And I see it didn't take you long to refill your plate."

Again Jared laughed, but before he could answer her, May and John appeared beside them.

"What's amusing, darling?" May asked.

"Laura used a witty metaphor," Jared answered, smiling.

"How nice," May warbled sweetly as she claimed Jared, slipping her arm through his.

"Enjoy your meal," Laura said to Jared and, taking John by the arm, marched away, hearing Jared's laughter behind her.

"Please, John. Let's take a brief walk outside," Laura said.

"Sure," John said.

Laura would rather have escaped quietly alone, but she didn't want to risk John's noticing anything in her behavior that might link her with Jared or May, so she said nothing. They took a short stroll on the narrow paved road leading out of town and sat on a wall beside the road, feeling the warmth of the night on their backs.

If there was such a thing as having a bad day in which you should have stayed in bed, Laura thought, this was her day. May Donnelly's appearance should have ended her concern over her strange feelings for Jared but it hadn't. You're infatuated with Jared, came the sudden horrific thought, and you're already in love with Bill. She shivered at the admission. Wasn't it the stuff novelists thrived on? Thank heaven it was nipped in the bud by May's appearance before she made a fool of herself.

"Cold?" asked John, having noticed her shiver. He drew off his jacket to drape it around her shoulders.

She managed to smile and murmur her thanks.

"I'd give a lot to know them," John said as he put his arm around her.

"My thoughts?" She laughed. His arm tightened on her shoulder. "No, you wouldn't," she said putting a finger up to his chin to lightly caress it. It was an artless gesture, and a spontaneous one, but to her dismay she heard John give a sigh and take her in his arms and in one quick movement plant his lips firmly on hers.

The headlights of a small white Porsche flashed on them as they kissed. Laura stiffened and broke the embrace. It looked like Jared at the wheel. She heard tires squeal around the bend in the road as the red taillights flashed out of sight. Was he so much on her mind that he was everywhere? Jared didn't have a Porsche. The man had bedeviled her.

She sighed. John, unfortunately, took her sigh to mean she had liked his kiss and started to repeat it. As he bent his head she turned hers and he withdrew. He kissed her lightly on the cheek.

"Friends?" he asked.

"I . . ." she began, but he interrupted her.

"It's all right, you don't have to explain."

John walked her back to the *pensión* and said good

night in the shadow of the trailing bougainvillea, reminding her of their proposed hike to the top of the mountain the coming weekend.

Back in her room Laura felt tired and confused and determinedly sat down to write a letter to Bill.

She took out her stationery and pen and began with a flourish . . .

"My Dearest Bill."

But a half hour later she had written not a single word more, and reluctantly, feeling depressed, she went to bed.

Chapter Four

In class Monday morning as he discussed the papers they had written, Jared was icily dry. He neither praised them nor condemned them but pointed out the ways to improve their style and content. He then asked them to write about a transforming experience in their lives. A new exercise, he told them. They could draw on what they had already written, and he named the students he wanted to continue with what they had started. Laura's name was not among them.

Laura kept her face turned to the window, staring at the stone facade of the opposite building.

"Are you listening, Miss Downes?" Jared's low voice intruded sharply. "Or dreaming?"

Laura's eyes sparkled with anger. "I heard you, Mr. Tanner," she said.

"Good. I expect results."

Jared dismissed them. Laura couldn't help but feel his presence as he left the room in the midst of the students who were plying him with questions about their papers. Outside she saw him climb into a waiting white sports car, a Porsche. May Donnelly, flawlessly dressed and radiant, was at the wheel. It *had* been Jared in the car driving past her and John Saturday night. Good. He had seen their kiss.

It was a relief to go to lunch with John and Susan, who were in a good mood. But after they discussed the hike up the mountain scheduled for Saturday, Susan surprised Laura by saying in an unexpectedly serious voice:

"I've met the most interesting man."

Laura gave her friend a questioning look. John smiled. Susan had never used that adjective to describe any man in the past; it had always been "that hunk" or "dream."

"Why is he so special?" Laura asked, raising an eyebrow.

"He's different," Susan replied, her eyes bright. "He's not like anyone I've ever met before."

"Even me?" said John, smiling.

"Even you, dreamboat," Susan said.

"Now that sounds like the Susan I know," teased Laura.

Susan was peeved. "The two of you think I'm never going to get serious, don't you?"

"Well, tell us about him," Laura said.

"He's an architect from London, here on business. He's not an artist. He's serious. Anyway, when you meet him, you'll know what I mean. He's got a level head."

"He's probably got a wife and six children back in England," Laura said half-seriously. It sounded to her as if Susan was being awed by an older man.

"Oh, Miss Priss, that's the first thing that comes into your head, isn't it?" Susan said, making a disapproving face.

"I just don't want you to get hurt," said Laura.

"By a mere man?" Susan countered. "You know me better than that." All three of them laughed.

Later, as Laura and Susan trudged back up the stairs to their rooms, Susan eyed Laura speculatively.

"Why don't you angle for him?" she asked on the threshold of Laura's room.

"Who?" asked Laura, thinking she was going to say John.

"Jared Tanner, of course," came the reply.

"Don't be silly," Laura said too quickly.

"I'm not as silly as you are. I can see what's going on. There were enough sparks on that dance floor the other night to burn the building down. He's interested in you. And you, my friend, despite all the interns in the world, are not exactly indifferent."

"Susan, please, I don't want . . ."

"If I were in your shoes, I'd put on my war paint and go fight for him. Don't let May Donnelly fool you. She's glamour plus, but blond fluff."

"Susan," Laura began, feeling her anger rise as she sat on the edge of her bed, "Mr. Tanner's life is not my concern nor is May Donnelly's. I don't care what they do, and I'd appreciate it if you wouldn't let yourself get carried away with any ideas. I'm engaged to Bill and intend to stay that way."

Susan rolled her blue eyes heavenward. "I guess I've been told. Oh, well, it's the tall oaks who fall with the mightiest thud. Just don't break any limbs."

Laura threw a pillow at her and, laughing, Susan left.

A fine mist was rising over the village as Laura made her way at dawn with John and Susan and eight other students to meet Eric and Maria Tabor and Jared in front of the café. Sleepily, they checked their satchels of food and flasks of water. There was a hushed air of expectancy. Only a few *señoras* were out at this hour, sweeping their doorsteps or bringing new-laid eggs home for breakfast. The plan was to hike up the mountain and on to the peak for a view of both sides of the island and to get back down before dark. Armed with flashlights and warm sweaters, they began their trek through the village to the base of the mountain.

As they crossed the stone bridge over the *torrente,* where only a small stream of water flowed over the rocks below, sheep ran from their approach, their neck bells clanging. They began climbing up from one terrace to the next, the thick twisted silver-gray trunks of the olive trees like abstract paintings. After twenty minutes Laura had to stop to adjust the pack straps over her shoulder. Her desert boots, which she had bought new before leaving New York, were a little tight and rubbing against her heels. She was afraid they would cause trouble before the day was over.

Hearing laughter, Laura glanced up ahead and saw the broad back and black-hatted figure of Jared talking to Eric and Maria. She sensed that he was as much at ease here as he was in the classroom. He was companionable with the students, but with a dignity that set him apart. He hadn't greeted her verbally, but she remembered with a trace of a smile the way he had touched his hat at the beginning of the expedition. Was it a peace offering?

She dismissed that train of thought and concentrated on the hike, which wasn't hard to do, as each new step brought a new view of the village, the clustered houses looking like small feudal castles. The orderly layout of the village, the interdependence of the land with the people was evident everywhere. The houses and terraces were built to last, to be passed on. There was no need to leave the village for jobs in a city. Everything was here for the continuity of life. Laura felt a surge of exhilaration. It was extraordinarily beautiful.

Laura, Susan, and John caught up to the others when Eric stopped to chat with a farmer he knew who was cleaning his already well-kept garden with a wooden rake.

"Buenos dias," Laura said to the farmer as she passed by him. The man stood back, smiling as he watched the group troop on upward. He had the solidity and serenity of the olive trees surrounding him.

As they came to the end of the terraces and the beginning of the real climb, a rugged ravine that led up the mountain, they separated into single file. The steep trail was obvious at first, marked by little piles of stones, but Laura could see how one could get lost if he didn't know what to look for. The trail, rocky and narrow, was arduous. Laura stopped to don her extra pair of socks and found herself bringing up the rear. As she started hiking again, she saw Jared turn and stop a minute, adjusting his hat and falling back a few places. Laura caught up to a few students behind him to hear him telling a pretty student about the Moors and Romans who had swept over these islands in conquest centuries ago.

"The Moors brought the olive trees and created the terraces," he was saying quietly. "You can also see their influence in the architecture and in the decorations on tiles and pottery. Some of the designs on the painted pottery were created five hundred years ago. They're still being used and are just as beautiful today as anything you'll find on the island. The Romans built the aqueducts and reservoirs that are still used."

"Is that what that sluice is that runs past our *pensión?*" the girl asked.

"That's right," said Jared. "There's another one east of the village."

Laura couldn't hear the next remark the student said to Jared, but whatever it was caused Jared to laugh lightly.

Eric and Maria, who had been in the lead, were now taking a rest by the side of the trail. Eric was leaning on a rock, occasionally puffing on a cigarette and letting it dangle from his lips in a precarious manner.

When Laura came up to them, she said lightly to them that she was sure he was going to set his beard on fire. His wife laughed and said, "Maybe he'll stop smoking then!"

"Never," Eric said, his blue eyes twinkling. "I'll create a new style in beards and you'll have to live with the foolishness of having married a half-bearded artist." Stroking his scraggly beard, he added, "I've wanted a goatee for a long time anyway."

Eric waved the next few students on. "Go ahead. If you get to a point that looks difficult, stop," he called to them, "and wait for me or Jared to catch up. These bones have to rest."

Laura saw that Jared had stopped a dozen yards up the trail, his hands on his hips, looking farther upward.

"Jared," Eric shouted. "Look at those clouds. Do you think it will rain?" His brow furrowed.

Jared came back down to them and, looking at the sky, stood assessing the situation.

"Maria," Jared said. "What do you say, rain or not?"

"It's possible," she answered him, shrugging. "We can take shelter in a sheep shed if it does."

"Wonderful," Eric said, grinning at his wife. "Ask a native what she thinks about the weather and you get philosophical advice to retire with the sheep in a shed."

Jared chuckled. "She gave the only possible answer, Eric. How many times have you seen clouds this time of year that produce nothing?"

"Oh, come on," said Eric, "you want me to be intelligent as well as an artist, that's too much!" he laughed. "That's why I tell my son to be an accountant. So he can deal with heavy matters like weather, statistics, and money!" He threw up his hands in a gesture of futility.

Maria laughed, sitting down beside her husband.

"Did you bring wine in that thing?" he asked his wife pointing to her dangling water pouch. "Or water?"

"What do you think?" she asked throwing him a glance, her short brown hair falling forward around her cheerful face.

"Water," he said, giving a grimace. "I would stake my life on it."

"Well, you guessed right," she said handing it over to him.

"Ech!" said Eric, making a face after taking a swallow of the water. "How I envy you your freedom, Jared. I bet none of your women treat you this way."

"I might be quite happy with water in my canteen," said Jared, smiling, "if the rest of my life were filled with the kind of wine you and Maria have together."

Maria flushed happily, but Eric made another exaggerated face.

"The words of a doomed man," he said brightly, putting his arm around his wife. "Get married and you think your worries are over, but they've just begun. Your wife rearranges your bedroom, your eating and drinking habits, and your morals all in one sweep!"

"I'll keep that in mind," said Jared, smiling.

Laura felt awkward, as if she were eavesdropping on a conversation she shouldn't hear, but as she started hiking up again, Jared silently joined her. Something in their chemistry was touched off when he came near, as if only they existed.

"No blisters yet?" he asked her finally.

"Not yet," she said, hardly conscious of the question. She felt tired, but she didn't want to admit her weakness to him. They'd been climbing steadily for an hour.

"Want to rest?" he asked as they neared a place where she saw others in the shade of a carob tree. John was there, too, watching them.

"No, not yet." There were no others on the rough path ahead. The climb was getting steeper every minute.

"Okay," he grinned. "We'll pioneer, then." She half hoped he would stop and she could regain her sense of herself.

She let her eyes slide over him briefly. He looked like a Spanish *gaucho* in a faded denim shirt and blue jeans, a leather sheepskin vest open in front, and the black-brimmed hat on his head. It made his dark looks fierce, piratical.

"Why don't you stop with the others?" she asked him.

"Want to get rid of me?" he asked her quietly.

"I have a feeling it wouldn't make any difference to you if I did or didn't." She looked at him and wished she hadn't. Their eyes met and locked into that feeling she couldn't explain to herself and made her stumble.

He took her by the arm, leading her to the side of the path where a small patch of tall grass grew near the rocks.

"The roughest part is coming next and it's straight up," he said. "Let's rest here."

Doubt was written all over her face.

"I'm not going to jump you in front of all the others, so relax." He adjusted his hat, his eyes coming lazily to meet hers, as he leaned against the rock while she sat on the soft grasses. "Did it ever occur to you, Laura, that it might be simpler for us both if you let me act naturally, out of courtesy? Your sudden switches from warmth to cold often seem like rudeness."

"I guess I never thought about it," she said, not looking at him. "If I've been impolite, I apologize, but I won't be a bit player in anyone's drama." A quick glance in his direction caught a wicked grin.

"What about a leading role?" he asked, adjusting his black hat so that it shaded his eyes.

Laura's stomach muscles knotted as warning signals went off in her head. He didn't mean it. Don't get caught in his trap. She wrenched her eyes from his face. He was so still, she looked back, slowly turning her head.

"Well," he asked softly, "yes or no?"

Laura stared at the ground. "Yes or no what? I've forgotten the question."

"I think you know, but the question frightens you." He smiled. "So does the answer."

Laura felt incredibly tense, but all the time she was aware of that deep warmth, of the blood singing in her veins. She leaned back and closed her eyes and let out a sigh. Spreading her long hair out around her shoulders to cushion the ground, she tried to rest. She felt an uncomfortable silence between them, and when she opened her eyes she found him watching her.

Suddenly she was amused. "All you need is a pair of six shooters to make your outfit complete," she said, smiling. "That hat does something for you."

"That's the closest you've come to saying something nice to me." He tipped his hat back. "It *was* a compliment, wasn't it?" He quirked an eyebrow at her.

"I suppose. Just like the kind you pay my writing efforts." She brought herself up to a sitting position, pulling on a blade of grass thoughtfully.

Jared looked surprised. "I admire your writing," he said. "You have a flair with words and are a sharp observer. Your short story was good."

"Although with a few flaws," said Laura, remembering his many written comments.

"If I had to read my own work as critically as I do yours, mine would have as many flaws," he replied.

"For some students you never have negative comments," Laura said, sitting up as the ground became too hard on her back.

"I'll tell you a secret, Laura," Jared commented. "I never offer much criticism to students I don't think can ever be good writers. For them writing can be therapy and any expression is good expression. It's only with the good writers that I try to point out flaws."

Laura laughed.

"I must be very good indeed," she said, drawing up her knees as some climbers passed by.

"Come on, lazy bones," Eric called to the two of them. "Time to get climbing again."

"Right," said Jared, picking up his pack and adjusting it to his back. He came over and put a hand down to help her up. Seeing several students approaching, including John, she wanted to refuse, but Jared ignored her hesitancy. As he pulled her easily up beside him the warmth of his hand sent a wave of emotion through her.

Jared immediately left to forge ahead with Eric, but John dropped back, giving her a suspicious look. As they climbed he talked about the views but Laura was quiet. She was just a few feet ahead of him in the single file when he asked her if she was enjoying her classes with Jared.

"They're fine," she answered, trying to sound off-hand.

"Well, don't seek his approval too much," he said pointedly.

"What do you mean?" she asked, stopping to face him and aware she was a little out of breath.

"You're playing with fire," he said. There was a sharpness to his voice she had never heard before.

"I'm not flattered by what you're implying," she said with equal sharpness and wheeled to press on up the trail ahead of him.

As she left him behind Laura felt annoyed. Could John see something she was unaware of? It wasn't possible to avoid Jared; why should he think there was anything special?

When they finally reached a point where there was nothing around them but jagged rocks and stubby growth, the whole group stopped to rest. An undulating but relatively flat surface lay before them, the last peak a half mile off in the distance.

Looking back, Laura could see the tiny village way below her: a postcard of tiled roofs, winding roads looking like footpaths, and clusters of miniature houses. At the rim of the mountain the blue Mediterranean stretched into the distance. Looking ahead she could see dark clouds touching the higher peaks. It was another world, where only sheep and grasses existed. She heard the students exclaiming over the view. A few sat down to take a rest and absorb the beauty. Many years ago, she remembered Jared telling them during a class, the Spaniards had planted wheat atop the mountain. Now the fields were simply an overgrazed sheep pasture. Laura wondered as she looked around how even the sheep could eke out their existence. She marveled that those ancient wheat farmers managed to meet their needs with such incredible industry, using everything around them including this high plateau, now so rugged and barren.

A student's voice broke into her thoughts, calling for Jared. Thirty yards ahead one of the women had slipped and twisted her ankle and couldn't go on. The group stopped in disarray. Eric and Jared hurried to where the girl was huddled. Laura dropped her pack and ran when she saw it was Susan. Jared was bending over her to examine the damage and then proceeded to bind the foot with a handkerchief, his face serious.

Susan's voice was shaky as she said, "I wasn't watching where I was going. Of all the luck!"

"Now we've got a problem," Eric said, stroking his beard.

Laura began mothering Susan, joking with her until she laughed at her predicament.

"You'll have to go down to the nearest farm where we can get a car to you," said Jared matter-of-factly to Susan.

"I was afraid of that," said Susan.

"I'll go with her," said Laura, glad to help Susan.

Jim, one of the students, volunteered to accompany them. Jared considered a minute, then thanked Jim and turned to Laura. "I think Jim and I will go down. If Susan needs to be carried, we'll be able to manage it easily enough. There's no need for you to go."

Laura wanted to argue with him, but Eric intervened, and he and Jared got into a discussion about which one of them should go back. Eric argued adamantly that he knew the farmers well and someone besides Maria had to stay with the students.

"And you remember the trail almost as well as I do," Eric added pointedly. His tired expression indicated he was ready to end his hiking. It was that, Laura thought, that decided Jared.

Jared helped Susan up and she found she could place some weight on her foot. With help she might be able to hobble down the mountain.

"I think I should go with her," Laura said, her concern for her friend written on her face.

"Absolutely not," said Susan. "If you think I'd let you come when I've got two men to lean on, you're crazy. I'm going to enjoy playing the helpless female for once." She threw Laura a playful wave. Laura felt Susan's words were meant to not spoil her trip, so she smiled and waved back as she watched her go.

"Do you think it's broken?" Maria asked Jared, when they had gotten out of earshot.

Laura listened for his answer. That had never occurred to her.

"No," he said. "She was tired. Her ankle will swell some, but she'll be all right with rest and an icepack."

"I didn't think she could have broken it," Maria said, "I was right behind her when she fell. But," Maria shrugged, "you never know what's going to happen on these trips." She pointed upward. "Right this minute, I'm more worried about rain than I was. The clouds are gathering." She looked at Jared.

Jared put his hand to his chin thoughtfully. "I think we won't try for the peak. We've lost time. Sound all right to you if we hike on another hour or so, eat, explore, and then begin down?"

"That's good," Maria said, brightening.

Laura was disappointed as she listened to their discussion.

Jared explained the new plan to everyone, adding, "When we get up there, I don't want anyone taking off alone. It's too easy to get lost."

Laura went back for her pack, adjusting it to her back, and joined the others as they started upward.

After forty minutes Jared stopped them in a large field. "We'll explore here and then head back," he said.

Laura could hear sheep trotting away from the sound of people, their bells making a low tinkle. The sun had all but disappeared behind the clouds.

Several of the eight students remaining wanted to go on to the peak. They didn't mind getting a little wet and they hated to have their hike curtailed, but Jared was firm, reminding them again the day was advancing rapidly and they still had to get back before dark.

"Storms in these mountains can be fierce," he pointed out, "and there's almost no place to go for cover."

John came up to Laura. "Come on. Let's have a look around," he said. She fell into step with him, but she hoped someone would join them. She saw Jared settling beside Maria on a rock. Several other students left to investigate the wheat fields. There had been a suggestion of possession in the way John had walked over to her. The feeling was soon erased as they left the others behind and began hiking toward the peak following the old stone trail.

Laura was enthralled with the wild landscape. Scrubby bushes and clumps of spiky grasses dotted the rough, rocky terrain. John started talking about the artists living in the village, a subject that never seemed to tire him. Laura, absorbed in her own musings, was barely conscious of what he was saying.

"You're not paying much attention," he said, after they had ambled on awhile.

"I'm sorry," Laura said, "I'm just too wrapped up in the hike. I don't want to miss anything."

"I noticed you didn't have much trouble talking to Jared back on the trail," he said.

Laura looked up quickly.

"Is that any of your business?" she asked, increasing her pace.

"Don't pull that lady routine on me." John said abruptly. "I saw you sprawled on the ground in front of him. It looked like an invitation if there ever was one."

Laura's eyes widened. "How can you say such a thing to me!" She jammed her hands in her pockets.

"Doesn't it bother you that he's May Donnelly's lover? Or are you hoping to get on his list? Maybe you want to become the romantic heroine in his next novel."

"I think you'd better go!" she said heatedly.

He stopped dead in his tracks, his lips compressed in a narrow line.

"If that's the way you want it. I only hope you don't regret it." He turned and left her standing on the trail.

She stared after him. Why was he so jealously possessive? She had given him no cause to be. She wished Bill were there to end her doubts and confusion. She tried to concentrate on him but could only bring to mind the photo she had of him; the rest of him seemed to have vanished. Although it was possible John would spread insinuating stories about her and Jared, she didn't think he was the type for that. Then his words came back to her: "He's May Donnelly's lover." So it was probably true. Of course, why else would May be here? The thought of Jared's using Laura rankled: aspiring writer losing her head over urbane novelist, losing more than her head too. She choked on the thought. If he . . . but why was she going on this way? They hardly had any relationship. Their exchanges were inexplicably disturbing, but not to be taken any more seriously than sudden violent storms.

Laura couldn't go back yet. Just the thought of seeing Jared right now was too disconcerting, and she needed to dispel the unpleasantness with John. She looked around her, and seeing an outcrop not too far off, she headed for it. Heedlessly, she picked her way over the rocks, beginning to regain some of her spirits. But the outcrop, which had seemed so close, was much farther away than it first appeared, and Laura began to feel guilty. When she finally arrived and scrambled up the rocky prominence, she had a wonderful view of the old wheat fields, but the peaks and valleys she had hoped might emerge were covered with clouds, and a mist was slowly rolling toward her.

Which way had she come? She hadn't remembered to put the little piles of rocks as markers on the path she had taken. The terrain looked the same in every direction. Deciding that valor was ninety percent risk, she started hiking down. A cool wind was blowing on her face, and it had become perceptibly darker. The path that led down from the rocky peak should begin about here. It was taking too long to find it. She stopped and took a good look around, searching for something in the landscape to jog her memory. Her mind was a blank as she took in the sameness all around her: rush grasses, odd boulders, the mist curling around them. She couldn't be lost! Panicked at the thought, she started walking again, trying to follow her instincts. Finally she saw what looked like a pile of stones on a rock. Giving a cheer, she headed for it only to discover it was unfamiliar. She reasoned that it was not the exact point of departure, but at least it was a marker, and she headed down the path. Thunder rolled behind her and she felt a few drops of rain.

Where was everyone, she wondered. Had they all forgotten her or become impatient and left her? It would be her own fault if they had, she knew, and wondered how Jared would react.

She walked wearily down the path. Where would she go if it rained? In the distance the lightning jagged straight down and the thunder echoed. She gave a start, remembering Jared's warning that storms in these mountains weren't simple affairs, and she understood why. The elevation made them closer, the low clouds right overhead made their impact ferocious. A cold fear gripped her. She could be up here all night, alone, waiting for the storm to pass or a search party to find her. She felt her hands tighten on the straps of her pack. She was hungry and tired, too tired to think straight. Her only thought now was to find shelter from the approaching blackness.

Bleakly she realized she must have wandered around for more than an hour. As she was trudging along she thought she heard her name called on the wind. She stopped. It must be her imagination. There was nothing but the thunder getting closer and the wind rising. Then she heard the familiar sound of the sheep bells. If she found them, she would find cover, hopefully in a shed. She followed the sound. The silly animals ran from her as she approached them. They weren't in a shed at all but were lying in indentations on the land. The rain wouldn't bother their thick woolly coats. She sat down, exhausted, the sheep beginning to settle farther away.

"Laura!" she heard it distantly again, but this time she knew it wasn't her imagination. Looking in the direction of the voice, she could dimly see a dark figure not too far away. She stood up, a feeling of relief flooding through her.

"Here I am!" she shouted.

Jared came running up to her. She could hear his hard breathing as he approached fast, surefooted over the rocks.

"What did you think you were doing?" he said as he came up to her, his face dark with anger. "Come on," he said, grabbing her hand, "we haven't a minute to lose."

"I'm sorry," she said on the edge of tears.

"So am I!" He held her hand tightly looking down to examine her face. "Are you all right?" he asked.

"Yes," she said.

"There's a cave not too far from here. We can take cover there," he said.

"Aren't we going down?"

"It's too late for that."

"But where are the others?" she asked, breathlessly following him.

"I sent them down. Did you expect everyone to risk themselves trying to find you with a storm coming up?"

"Of course not. I just thought they'd take cover too."

"You've been gone two hours, woman. The moment you didn't get back with John, I sent them all on their way and then I tried to find you. It wasn't easy."

"I . . ." she wanted to apologize but frustration confused her and she blurted, "Anyone could get lost up here."

"You don't have to tell me that," he said firmly. He turned to look at her a moment, his eyes fiery. "Just hope I can still find the cave."

He plunged ahead, glancing around him as if trying to read the rocks for signs. The dark clouds seemed to be rolling toward them, enveloping the mountains and hiding their rugged shapes. The thunder crashed like an earthquake at their backs. Laura became silent too, following Jared as rapidly as her exhausted legs would take her. It was beginning to rain and the cold drops seemed to penetrate her skin like needles.

Jared stopped a minute as if to get his bearings, his black hat shadowing his face. Laura was breathing hard. A fear came into her that he too was lost, but then he abruptly charged forward again.

"Over here," he said.

They came upon a rocky outcrop. The cave was very small, dug out from time to time by sheepherders who had gotten trapped up here as they were. There was squatting and lying room only and a place near the front of a rock overhang where fires had been built. Pieces of blackened wood were still in the circle of rocks and someone had piled a stack of wood to one side.

Squatting, Jared took off his pack and stripped to the waist, his bare, browned chest gleaming damply in the half-light. His muscles rippled. Laura longed suddenly to touch him, towel him dry, hold him.

"Stay here," he said and went out into the worsening storm.

Laura sank back against the rock wall. The cave was dark and so small there was barely room for them and their packs. It flashed through her that she would be spending the night here with Jared, listening to that storm outside, a few inches separating her from him. A great weakness rolled through her, coupled with a warm excitement; she sternly suppressed them both, and turned her attention to finding some kindling for the fire.

A crack of thunder made her jump.

Her heart raced and she poked her head out, but found the rain and the darkening sky so dense she couldn't see more than a few yards in front of her.

"Jared?" she called, getting no answer in return. She began putting sticks in the circle of rocks for a fire to keep busy. Her blue sweater was damp, but she hadn't the energy to take it off. She would freeze without it anyway, she reasoned.

Jared came back bringing several rough, twisted

logs with him. His body glistened with drops of rain and a little trickle of water ran off his hat.

"Oh, good," he said. "You've collected kindling." He started a fire, blowing on it until it was crackling. Carefully, he put a log on, feeding it slowly. He hung his clothes around and pulled his sheepskin vest over his bare chest. He finally sat back, propping himself against the rough wall, taking off his hat.

"We have an interesting way of coming together in unexpected places," he drawled, looking at her.

"It wasn't planned," she said tiredly.

"Not by us," he answered quietly.

She felt warmed by the fire, but just as quickly a chill went through her.

"You better take your sweater off," he said, seeing her shiver.

"I'm all right," she said, a feeling of reluctance to shed anything in the intimate situation. She glanced at him, not trusting those dark knowing eyes, but realized she was being unreasonable. She took off her sweater and hung it on a rock point to dry, drawing closer to the fire. She hugged her knees and rested her head on them, trying to get warm.

"You're still cold," he said.

"A little," she admitted.

"There's a light blanket in my pack, and a small pot to boil water. You'll also find some instant coffee. If your jeans are wet, take them off and wrap yourself in the blanket."

She glanced warily at him. That would be inviting trouble, she told herself.

"Laura," he said softly, "I'm not a ravager of helpless women, although I'd question your helplessness. I've more control than that and a greater sense of both who I am and what I want. I'll close my eyes, if that's what's bothering you."

She took in a deep breath, putting her hands up to push her hair away from her fire-flushed face.

"This is no ordinary situation," she said.

"It isn't going to be a typical night for either of us, but we can make it comfortable. Would you feel more comfortable with John?"

"Yes," she said honestly, "but you're not John." As if to punctuate her words, a clap of thunder and a hiss of lightning startled her.

"No, I'm not." He reached forward in the little space to retrieve his pot and put some water on to boil.

"Did you bring a cup?" he asked.

"No, just this canteen and I'm afraid it's half empty."

He laughed. "We've no shortage of water, have we." He made a cup of coffee, lacing it lightly with cognac from a small flask. He took a drink and handed it to her. "Drink this. It'll warm you."

She took the cup, acutely aware of the act of sharing. His fingers lightly brushed hers in the exchange. The cognac in the coffee was strong and burned like fire in her empty stomach.

"I'm hungry," she said.

He pulled out what was left of a loaf of bread and some cheese. "Not much, but we won't starve." He handed her a sandwich.

She ate slowly, taking small bites with the coffee, and beginning to feel better. She was slightly dizzy.

"You seem to be making a habit of rescuing damsels

in distress." She tossed her head back, her long hair flowing down her back.

"I hate to disillusion you," he said, "but I'm just a man," he leaned forward, ". . . stranded with a lovely woman and enjoying it."

Laura forgot the moment's relaxation as wariness swept through her.

"Don't look that way every time I say something complimentary," Jared went on. "How can I make it easy for you? By remaining silent?"

Her feelings were too complicated to give him an answer. She shivered and reached around to feel her sweater, but it was still damp.

Jared opened his knapsack and brought out the light wool blanket. "Not much," he said as he drew it gently around her shoulders, "but it's dry." She saw his eyes drawn to her lips as he tucked the blanket under her chin, and made the mistake of looking up; the desire she saw in his eyes made her gasp. He sat back against the wall of the cave drawing her with him. She pulled back, but his hands and arms were firm.

"No," she said.

"No," he echoed her flatly. "Don't worry, Laura. It's all right." He pulled her head against his chest and stroked her hair like a child. "Go to sleep," he whispered. "I'm tired and cold myself."

He put his arms around her, finally persuading her to relax against him. She could feel his heart beating evenly under the sheepskin vest. In his arms she felt safe, while the rain cascaded down outside and the thunder and lightning did their worst. He laid his cheek against her head gently, stroking her arm and back until he too relaxed and they drifted into sleep.

Sometime toward morning she awoke to find herself entwined in his arms. In the night they had slid into a prone position. Laura turned her head up to look at Jared, shocked with the feeling of the rightness of their being together. She could feel his warm breath on her face.

"Laura?" he questioned softly.

"Yes . . ." she said slowly.

He brought his lips down to hers and kissed her gently. Slowly the kiss turned into a passionate exploration. Laura felt herself melting toward him like warm honey. His hands caressed her skin beneath her shirt, gently tracing her breasts to tease her nipples, then running down the front of her body. She groaned beneath his lips, bringing her hands beneath his vest to touch his sleep-heated skin, running her hands over the muscles of his chest. A thigh possessed her; an urgency rushed through her body, she wanted more. He stopped, pressing his lips against her cheeks, his breath jagged, then he slowly released her.

"I'm only human, Laura, I have to stop," he whispered roughly.

He took her hand and placed it near his heart. "See how wildly it's beating," he asked, smiling. He turned from her and sat up, letting her hand go.

Laura stiffened, feeling both a frustrated desire and embarrassment.

"I'm sorry," he said thickly. "You're young, and I care about you, but I don't seduce every woman I meet."

"I didn't expect you to go on," she answered.

"That's the hell of it," he said.

Laura turned away, stretching on her stomach, her head on her arms.

"It's dawn," he said quietly and started to rekindle the blackened fire. When he had gotten it going, he put the little pot of collected rainwater on to boil and crawled out of the cave.

Laura struggled with her feelings, unable to decide what was right or wrong. Abruptly he came back and she got up, crawling out of the cave herself, avoiding his eyes.

"Don't go far," he warned gently. She could see why. A heavy rolling mist obscured everything. Would they spend another day up here together? She felt an absurd gaiety at the thought. They had only coffee and cold bread and cheese. She gave a little laugh. Bread and water: prison fare, yet somehow with Jared it was enough. She returned, crouching outside the entrance, the aroma of coffee starting her stomach going. He silently passed the coffee to her. She cupped her hands around its warmth.

"Would you pass me my sack?" she asked, handing him the empty cup, which he refilled.

Laura found her hairbrush in her sack and began vigorously trying to untangle her long hair. Jared was quietly watching her movements.

"You're a beautiful woman," he said softly. "Even in the morning."

His liquid tone of voice thrilled her. She tremblingly replaced her brush and, rummaging, found an uneaten orange. She handed him half of it, through the opening of the cave.

"I won't bite, come on in here. It's warmer and dry. I've an aversion to being fed like a lion in a cage."

She finally crawled in, sitting in front of the fire and spreading her hands over it. He leaned back. He had put on his clothes and had even given his hair a smoothing.

"Will it clear?" she asked him as they split what was left of the bread and cheese.

"Probably."

Unsettled by his silence, she said too quickly, "I'm not a tease. I didn't mean to let anything happen."

"I know."

"How soon will we be able to leave?" she asked, reaching for her sweater.

"I'll see." He crawled out to survey the scene.

"Come out and take a look," he called back. He was standing with his hands on his hips as she emerged. The mist was rolling back in waves and the sun was streaming in separate rays across the wet landscape. They could hear the sheep moving not too far off.

"We could even make it to the peak." He turned to her smiling.

Laura's heart disobediently fluttered at the thought.

His face became expressionless as he bent down to retrieve their packs. "Let's go," he said, pushing on his black hat.

"Home?" she asked tentatively.

"Home," he repeated drily.

Laura followed him silently, wishing she could penetrate his reserve. She looked at his back, her eyes drawn to him like a magnet. Mentally, she caressed the broad shoulders, slowly traveling down to his strong legs, the legs that had pressed against her, the thigh that had drawn her close to him this morning. There was an ache inside her. As if he could sense her eyes on him, he stopped and turned to watch her progress. She was startled by the penetration of his look as she drew closer, stopping close to him. He reached out and took her hand in his. She smiled at him with unexpected joy.

"We'll take our time," he said softly.

She gave him a puzzled look. Take their time going down? What did he mean?

"Yes," she said hesitantly, "it's so beautiful."

He flashed her a quick smile, his eyes lighting up. He dropped her hand. Then laughing softly, he started hiking.

"Yes," he said. "It's beautiful . . . and we'll take our time."

Chapter Five

An hour later, when they were halfway down, they saw a small group of climbers approaching. As they came nearer, Laura saw someone wave. May Donnelly, Eric, a male student, and a villager advanced on them.

"Jared!" May's high lilting voice called. "We were all so concerned about you. And Laura," she said as an afterthought, examining Laura.

"We're fine," said Jared as May slipped her arm through his and planted a light kiss on his cheek.

"You're grizzly," she said lightly.

The others with her were relieved to see Laura and Jared. Eric put an arm around each of them, smiling broadly. "I'm so glad to see you two," he said. "You don't even look wet. How did you stay dry?"

"Jared found a cave and we built a fire," Laura answered promptly.

"Oh, how cozy," May said looking at Jared. "I'm so glad you're all right. I knew you would be, though."

"Is that why you began climbing the mountain?" Jared said to May, an amused smile on his face. "Because you weren't worried?"

May's laugh was light and thin. "You know I was worried, silly. Why else would I don jeans and boots to stumble over these horrid rocks? But now it's all over, isn't it?"

Laura was glad when they finally got down to the road. May's car was parked on the side and she offered Laura and the student a ride back to the *pensión*.

After waving good-bye to Eric and the villager, Laura sat huddled in the back of May's car not able to think and not wanting to. The student was forcing conversation about their adventure, asking Jared questions. Laura's stomach muscles contracted, but Jared kept the answers short and impersonal.

May launched into nonstop chatter about her modeling activities, which included being photographed on the beach in Pollensa, a village on the other side of the island. Laura breathed a low sigh of relief when they arrived at the *pensión,* only to realize from the curious stares and teasing of some of the students that her adventure was far from over. Answering a few questions as lightly as she could, she hastened up to her room.

Susan was not to be put off, however, and seemed to have recovered from her twisted ankle.

"Well! Well!" she said when they were alone together in Laura's room. "You do spring surprises!"

"Susan," Laura said, "stop it. I've had enough. It could have happened to anyone."

"But it didn't," Susan said. "It happened to you and Jared. I couldn't have done better myself."

Laura groaned. She was back in the real world and the real world would believe what it wanted. She fell on her bed, exhausted. "Susan, I need a hot shower and sleep. Would you go away, please?"

Susan stopped short. "Can I help?" she asked.

"Yes. Everybody is leering at me. You can help by acting normal," Laura said.

"Don't worry," Susan replied, coming up and squeezing her shoulder. "I'm on your side." She left, and Laura let out a long sigh.

That evening Laura paced her room like a caged lioness. She was appalled by what was happening to her. Jared was becoming too important a part of her life. When she tried to focus on Bill, it was like looking through a mist: physically and emotionally he was distant, unclear, muted. Memories of him stirred no emotion other than sadness.

Yet that couldn't be, shouldn't be at any rate. For more than a year she'd thought of her future in terms of being Bill's wife; her parents had encouraged those thoughts; Bill certainly expected it. And he was a fine, decent man who loved her. How could she endanger all that for a man who seemed to follow every kiss by going off on the arm of a blond model? She laughed sardonically and kicked her hiking shoes under the bed.

It was madness. Jared Tanner was a good writer but vain, arrogant, and uncaring of women—who for him were mere playtoys for an evening's romp. But then why didn't he on the mountain . . . ? Why did he make her feel . . . ?

No! Those questions only fed an infatuation that had to end. Her future was settled.

But why couldn't she *feel* more for Bill? Had she

ever felt for him what she did sometimes for Jared? Damn! Well, feelings weren't all there was to love; there had to be respect and trust and common interests. Still, feelings had *some*thing to do with it and she wished she could re-create the warm feelings she knew she usually had for him.

She finally sat down and wrote a long letter to Bill. Although she wanted to be totally honest, she recognized that she herself didn't yet know what her feelings were, so without naming Jared she told Bill she was becoming confused and uncertain, that her future no longer seemed so clear, that living on Mallorca was having a profound effect on her. As she wrote, some of her affection for Bill was revived and she even began to write about her climbing the mountain, but abruptly stopped and discarded the page. If she wanted to stop the madness, there were some stories she had to forget.

In the next few days Laura endured teasing from a few of the students—quips like "Was it true what Eric Tabor said about the magic of the mountain?"—but she was able to handle them. Instead of becoming rigid and prudish she simply gave each one a Mona Lisa smile, which neither admitted nor denied anything. It was the best she could do.

If Jared was aware of the students' speculation about their night, he didn't show it. In the classroom he was professionally distant, giving no cause for rumor or gossip. There were no glances in her direction or unexpected smiles in the village. Laura was grateful but also a little hurt. He seemed to be avoiding her. Her mind told her she should be grateful but her heart disagreed. She was still unnaturally conscious of his presence, and when he was around, her eyes leaped to him, as though he were the magnetic north and she the compass. But she, like he, kept her distance.

Four days later Laura was confronted by a student outside her room.

"Miss Downes?" the young woman said. "May I speak to you?"

"Of course, Sheila," Laura replied as she was about to enter her room. "Come on in."

As Laura set her books down on her desk she wondered what Sheila wanted. Sheila was a small dark-haired girl, a sophomore at Darrow and a student in both of Laura's writing courses. She had seemed to be enjoying herself tremendously here at the Institute. She remained standing shyly at the entrance to Laura's room.

"Please sit down," Laura said and went to close the door for privacy. It was one of her jobs to counsel the students, but usually she saw them in the semiprivate space she used off the dining room as her office.

Sheila sat down in the one easy chair and began twisting her shoulder-length hair nervously with her hand at one shoulder.

"Now," said Laura, seating herself on her bed. "What can I do for you?"

Sheila looked at Laura doubtfully.

"Nothing, I guess," she said.

"If nothing else I can listen," Laura said encouragingly.

Sheila's expression had slowly changed from doubt to misery and as Laura watched, her chin began to tremble, and she was clearly fighting back tears.

"Please," Laura said gently. "Just go ahead and talk."

Again the girl was silent, still struggling both with whether to speak or to control her emotions. Finally she lowered her head and hid her face in her hands. She let out a huge sigh. Then she looked up at Laura with wistful defiance.

"I think I'm in love," she said softly.

Laura almost laughed, so surprised was she by the anticlimactic announcement. Laura had feared a disease or dishonesty, not love.

"It could be worse," Laura said with a soft smile.

"I don't think so," said Sheila.

"Being in love shouldn't be a problem for you," said Laura.

"I'm in love with Jared Tanner," Sheila announced, again in misery.

Laura felt her own heart skip a beat.

"With . . . does he return your love?" Laura said, aware of the irony in the situation.

"I . . . I don't know what's happening," Sheila burst out with sudden passion. "One minute I think he cares for me and the next he's so cold. Some days he makes me feel like I'm the only woman in the world who could make him happy and then he flirts with someone else. But I'm in love with him and I just don't know what to do about it. . . ."

Sheila stared blankly at Laura a moment more and then burst into tears, lowering her face again into her hands.

Laura didn't know whether to laugh or to cry with her. She was both angry at Jared for apparently leading Sheila on, ashamed of herself for being as much a foolish victim as Sheila, and relieved that with this new evidence of the real Jared she might more easily free herself from her own infatuation.

She went to Sheila and, sitting on the arm of the easy chair, put her arm around her and wordlessly tried to comfort her. Sheila's shoulders were shaking with her sobs and she was making loud sniffling noises that would have been comic were they not an expression of suffering.

"And he's so *beautiful*," Sheila sobbed out and again Laura had the incongruous urge to laugh, as if Sheila were parodying everything Laura had been dimly feeling and thinking.

After another half-minute Sheila took the tissue Laura offered her and blew her nose and wiped away the tears. Laura returned to sit on her bed and listened to Sheila pour out her story.

"When I asked him about my poetry, he didn't criticize it at all and said he thought there were a lot of good lines and to keep writing, and when a group of us were sitting at his table in the café I could tell he wanted to look at me and be alone with me but he was too polite, and at the pool at the Hotel Mallorquin when I did find him alone, he was moody and didn't want to talk. I've tried to make it easy for him, you know, being where he would be. One day I bumped into him outside his house on the *Puig* and he kissed me, but then he withdrew and became indifferent and I don't know what to think."

Laura sat silently for a moment, waiting to see if Sheila wanted to go on, and then asked.

"Has he ever . . . said anything to encourage you?"

"He . . . I handed in six love poems and he said he thought they were expressed with feeling."

"But . . . I mean when he kissed you, what did he say?" Laura asked, feeling repelled by her own question, yet knowing it was her job to get the facts in order to help counsel Sheila.

"Oh, I don't want to talk about it," Sheila said with sudden irritation. "I don't know if I'm just inexperienced in these things or I'm missing something. He certainly knows how to hurt."

"How . . . has he hurt you?"

"He's cruel. I mean you just don't kiss someone and then ignore them, do you?"

"I don't know," said Laura.

"I like to think he's holding himself back because I'm only a student and he's older. I'm *sure* he's attracted to me."

When Sheila again lapsed into silence, Laura stood up and walked slowly to her window and looked at the towering mountain to the east of the village. It seemed to lean against her now almost like a living force.

"I can sympathize with you, Sheila," she said, still staring at the mountain. "It's difficult with a strange man . . . in a strange land . . . to know . . . what's happening."

"Would you speak to him, Miss Downes?" Sheila burst out. "Let him know how I feel and find out why he's being so cold?"

Again Laura didn't know whether to be amused or miserable.

"Of course," she replied, turning. "I'll speak to Mr. Tanner."

"Some of the girls think he's a cold fish, but I *know* that's not true. He has to be discreet. Don't you think so?"

"Yes, Sheila, I think you're right."

"Thank you for listening and for offering to help me."

"I haven't done that yet, Sheila," said Laura, coming over to Sheila, who had stood to leave. "Remember, it may be that he doesn't want to see you. You must face that possibility too."

"You mean he's . . . you mean Miss Donnelly, don't you." She sighed, then continued. "Yes, I know, but it's the uncertainty I can't stand."

"I'll see what I can do."

When Sheila had left, Laura went again to her window to stare at the dark purplish tint of the face of the mountain. As near as she could tell, Sheila was being foolish, but it only seemed to confirm that Laura herself was only a slightly older fool. She wasn't sure she could speak to Jared about Sheila—it seemed too much an invasion of his privacy—and hoped Sheila would become aware of her folly without anyone else having to spell it out. But in the next two days of classes Laura found she couldn't approach Jared about Sheila. He seemed distant to all the students.

Three days later she received a letter from Bill that was written before he'd gotten her long one to him, which left her feeling uneasy. His letter was filled with plans and anecdotes to the old Laura he knew so well. She wasn't sure that woman still lived.

That evening she took a short walk along the narrow road outside the village to clarify her thoughts. There was little traffic at night. She sat down on the old stone wall watching the first stars appear in the sky, feeling low in spirits. She wondered if she was letting the exotic landscape and culture stimulate her imagination so as to exaggerate her reaction to Jared. Certainly that was what had happened to Sheila.

She turned her head as she heard someone approaching.

"Not lost again, are you?" Jared's voice startled her.

"Just lost in my thoughts," she said. It was the first real exchange between them since they had come down the mountain. He stood very close to her, seeming to watch the stars with her.

"Care for coffee with me?" he asked. "I'd like to talk to you."

She hesitated.

"You're not afraid to talk to me, are you?" he asked.

It was a challenge. "Of course not," she said, looking up into his shadowed face. "In fact, I'd like to talk to you," she added, thinking of Sheila.

He reached for her hand, but when she refused to take it, he laughed softly.

"Come on, then," he said.

She walked uneasily beside him, but as he turned into his own terrace, she blinked and stopped.

"I thought you meant the café," she said.

"This is better," he said. She knew she should leave, yet she wanted to be with him. She looked around to see if anyone was watching.

"Guilty feelings?" he laughed. "I've had students for coffee before, and they didn't hesitate to come in."

"Yes, I'm sure they didn't," she said and walked slowly up the three remaining steps to his door.

Following, Jared opened it to allow her entrance and switched on the light inside.

The room was spare and clean and very Spanish. A few dark wooden chairs stood to one side of the room and a desk was in one corner. In the center was a fireplace with glowing coals and a sporadic curl of flame indicating an earlier fire. In front of it was a red-and-black Mallorquin rug. The bookcase next to his desk was only half-filled with books, the other half of the shelves taken up with piles of manuscripts. A typewriter sat squarely in the center of the desk with a single pile of papers neatly stacked beside it. Jared moved off to the kitchen where she could hear him putting on a pot of coffee.

Laura lowered herself onto a cushion that lay in front of the fire and continued her perusal of the room. A jacket, one she had often seen him wear, hung carelessly over the back of the desk chair, and she saw his hiking boots tucked under the desk. It was a man's room with few concessions to decor, except for an incongruous vase of orange flowers over the fireplace.

Jared stood in the kitchen doorway, observing her.

He had taken off his jacket and leaned against the doorjamb. The sleeves of his brown velour shirt were pushed up and it was open at the neck.

"A woman's touch," he said following her gaze to the flowers on the mantelpiece.

Laura returned her eyes to stare into the fire. May Donnelly's touch, he didn't need to tell her.

He turned back into the kitchen.

"Would you like cognac?" he called to her.

"No, thanks," said Laura. Feeling restless, she got up to look into the kitchen. Jared was pouring himself a small glass of cognac in front of a cupboard well stocked with various drinks and fixings. The kitchen was spare and simple too, crockery neatly piled on the open shelves. She had expected to see the sink piled with pans and dirty dishes, but it was clean. There was a small refrigerator and a wooden table covered with a red woven cloth and several chairs pushed beneath it. The red tiled floor gleamed.

As if reading her mind, he turned to her and said, "A little lady from the village comes in three times a week to keep me orderly." He flashed her a smile and lifted his glass. *"Salud!"*

Laura was standing in the doorway, not wanting to venture forward. She had taken off her sweater and left it by the fireplace. She was wearing a bright pink knit shirt and as Jared's eyes roamed over her she was conscious that it displayed her womanly curves.

"Why did you invite me here?" she asked.

With one hand around his globelike glass of cognac he stood watching her. When the coffeepot began sending out hissing sounds he put his glass down and began pouring two fragrant cups of coffee.

"Milk or sugar?" he asked.

"Both, please," she said, aware that he was avoiding her question.

He opened the refrigerator and fixed their coffees.

"It seemed a good opportunity," he answered her finally. "We don't have many without a hundred eyes all around, do we?" As he handed her a cup he smiled. "Let's go in by the fire."

Laura seated herself on a cushion, putting her coffee down on the hearth before her. After taking a seat in an easy chair opposite her, Jared leaned back and gazed at the bright embers. There was an unresolved silence that Laura felt impelled to break.

"There's something I think I should talk to you about," she said.

"Oh?"

"Sheila Watson."

"Sheila Watson?"

She looked at him meaningfully, but he didn't react.

"One of your students," she added.

"I know, but what's the problem? She's doing passing work."

"She's in love with you."

"Ah," said Jared, scowling and getting to his feet. "And I am to blame."

"I didn't say that," said Laura. "Only that she loves you and that she isn't . . . certain how you feel about her."

Jared swung around to stare down at her.

"I don't lie, Laura," he said harshly. "If I'm attracted to a woman I let her know it, as . . ." he lowered his voice and gentled it, ". . . as I've let you know. I've done everything possible to make it clear to Sheila Watson that she should leave me alone."

"Including kissing her . . . ?" Laura asked coldly.

"Kissing her?" Jared snapped back. "Is that what she says?" Jared shook his head slowly. "I've certainly been aware that Sheila has had a fantasy-filled crush on me. And I admit, I did tease her about it when we bumped into each other on the beach . . ."

Laura sat still, staring into her still untouched coffee.

"Look, Laura," Jared went on. "I realize that my published attitudes toward women hardly inspire confidence. Nor the gossip columns of the last year, nor that article in *People* magazine I saw some of the students with."

She didn't reply but remained looking into the fire, feeling saddened by his having to defend himself.

"I came to Mallorca to get away from all that," Jared continued. "I wrote *The Female of the Species* out of a bitterness from a failed love and exaggerated all my feelings for effect. Then I let the media distort the reality of my social life because I didn't give a damn. But I'm not playing with you, Laura," he added with intensity. "I'd like to see you. If you'll let me, I want to court you openly."

His unexpected words jolted Laura and she looked sharply up at him.

"That's ridiculous! You can't expect me to believe you." She got up, nearly upsetting her cup of coffee. "I don't even know why I let you talk me into coming here." She gestured with her hand in agitation.

"You're still not answering me," he said watching her intently.

"I . . . I've got to go," she said in a low voice and started to move toward the door, but before she had even pivoted Jared moved in to stop her.

"You're not going anywhere until we get a few things straight." Jared's hands closed tightly on her arms.

"Please, Jared," Laura said as she tried to twist free of his grasp.

"I can't accept the fact that you came here only to tell me the tale about Sheila Watson. The whole institute would *know* I'd been pursuing Sheila and you'd have heard about it. You didn't have to talk to me about Sheila. So why did you come? I've been clear about why I invited you here, now I'd like the same honesty from you."

"I . . ." Laura swallowed hard, running her tongue over her suddenly dry lips, and put her hands on Jared's chest to keep him at a distance.

"I'm waiting, Laura," Jared's eyes were mocking her lightly and a smile began to curl at the corners of his sensuous mouth.

Laura's hands felt hot against his chest and she wanted to withdraw them, but needed the reassurance of having the barrier.

"I wish I could hate you," she finally said, a shiver running down her back. "I'm afraid . . ." The air around them had become electrically charged. Laura turned her face away from his probing eyes. "It's a stupid physical attraction . . . I must go." She made an effort to pull away from him, but Jared merely brought her up against him. She could feel his warm breath against her cheek, his arms tight around her waist.

"Look at me," he said softly.

Laura reluctantly brought her eyes up to his, her hands still between them.

"You can deny me with your words, but I'm not convinced." Jared brought his lips down to hers in a demanding kiss that left her knees weak. Slowly her arms slipped around his neck in submission, one hand curling into his thick black hair. She leaned into him, fusing herself against him as his lips and tongue explored the tenderness of her mouth. When he finally released her lips to trail hot kisses along her jawline to the sensitive curve of her neck, Laura was breathless.

"Admit it, Laura . . . you feel it too," he whispered, bringing his face close to hers, his eyes suffused with desire.

"No," she murmured. "I . . . I've made a commitment . . . to Bill. It . . . this . . ."

"Your head may have made a commitment," Jared said to her softly, "but not the rest of you." He kissed her again, more gently, and when he released her lips he held his face only inches away, his eyes glowing into hers. "I see your uncertainty about me, about your feelings, and I can see why you would hesitate— the age difference, your engagement—but you can't help yourself either, can you?"

Laura felt herself teetering on the brink of the most momentous decision of her life. The room was spinning dizzily. Jared's face swimming nearer and then away, only his dark gleaming eyes remaining steady.

As in a dream Laura realized Jared was leading her to the cushions on the floor, leaning her back, slowly, lovingly, sweeping her long chestnut hair away with his hand and then gently holding her face. His mouth began another descent to claim what was his.

"Jared . . . no," she said even while her body was clinging to his.

"Don't you know that I feel the same thing you feel?" he asked, his eyes meeting hers. Their breath mingled before he kissed her. Laura lost her self-awareness and let herself arch into him. His hands moved urgently over her body, intimately caressing her soft curves.

"Laura . . ." he whispered hoarsely, teasing her mouth with his tongue. "Stay with me." His hands freed an aroused breast and gently played with the hardened nipple. "I want you and you want me . . ."

Laura brought her hand to his wrist to stop his teasing fingers. "Jared . . . stop . . . please, I can't."

Jared laughed softly in her ear as he nibbled. "I can't stop, Laura . . . I need you now."

A sharp rapping noise at the door machine-gunned into their consciousness and Laura was aware that someone had been knocking even before. The room slowly stopped spinning for her. She heard Jared swear under his breath as he too finally heard the insistent rap.

"Who is it?" he called.

"Jared, darling, it's me, May."

Jared's face closed. He looked at Laura, who was still somewhat overwhelmed at the momentous cliff-edge she'd just been walking. Now the precipice was gone, but she felt herself sinking into some soft, ugly bog.

Jared took in a deep breath, his hand tensely gripping Laura's arm. She closed her eyes against his face.

"It's not what it seems," he whispered. Running a hand through his hair, he got slowly to his feet and went over to the door. He waited for Laura to pull herself together, buttoning her blouse with shaking hands. She quickly pulled on her sweater. Then he opened the door. May stood there a minute, a grim look appearing on her face when she saw Laura seated by the fire. May's eyes flicked coldly from one to the other.

"I didn't know you had someone here. I'm sorry." She gave them a hard smile and walked in through the door, without any apparent intention of retreating. Her eyes glittered, but she quickly composed herself. She was immaculately gorgeous in a white pantsuit, red shirt, matching shoes. She walked over to the desk.

"I brought back your manuscript. I finished reading it this evening. It's so wonderful, I couldn't wait to tell you." She smiled sweetly at Jared.

Laura put her cup aside and slowly got up to go. She was beginning to realize that what had just happened—and had almost happened—was still, for Jared, apparently only a minor fling in his full life.

"I'm just leaving," she said evenly, but Jared put a restraining hand on her arm to stop her.

"We were having coffee, May," he said, although casting a riveting look at Laura. "Can I offer you a cup?"

"Why, of course, darling."

Laura freed her arm from Jared.

"I'm afraid I have to go," she said numbly to Jared.

"Laura . . ." Jared began.

She smiled at May and, with a magnificently neutral glance at an agitated Jared, she quietly left.

Chapter Six

Laura cut her class with Jared the next morning. She didn't want to face him just yet, let him think whatever he liked. She shut herself in her room, going down for meals late to avoid most of the students. She needed time to gather her self-control and decide what to do. Every time she thought of her evening with Jared, of May discovering her there in his house like a thief, her heart gave a flutter and she blushed hotly. The man had no principles. She had no doubt that if she had stayed there and May hadn't come, she would have given in to the tide of emotion he so easily evoked in her.

She tried to concentrate her straying mind on her writing. Working furiously, she let words spill out on paper unheeded. She chose a character, a woman, and let her express all the emotions warring within herself: the desire, the fear, the loneliness even among friends, of hiding the deepest tides running in one's own heart. It gave her strength. When she finished, she felt calmer and she set it aside. She would turn it in to Jared. Good or bad, it didn't matter. It was honest. He had wanted papers that expressed the students' own reactions to being here in Spain. He'd get it.

Susan came in to see why she had missed classes. Laura said she had needed a day to get her work together, that she was behind in her work for Professor Johnson. Susan accepted her explanation without question.

"You *must* meet Bob," Susan said, sitting on Laura's bed. "He's not gorgeous to look at, but he's wonderful."

"I'd like to," said Laura.

"Don't be condescending, Laura Downes. Did I tell you he only arrived three weeks ago? This time something clicked right from the start. I feel right with him."

"It's awfully fast, Susan," Laura commented, staring at her.

Susan returned her look levelly. "This is different. He's mature. He takes me seriously. This time I've met my match."

Laura noted the dreamy expression on Susan's face, and worried. Susan had been "in love" many times, but she had always appeared buoyantly in control.

"I think the mountain's cast its spell on you."

"You don't believe that hocus-pocus, do you?" Susan retorted. "I heard Eric Tabor's story—he'd weave a tale about any place he loved. Come and meet Bob. I'll be at the café with him tonight. Please . . ."

Laura promised she would and Susan turned to leave.

"Oh, before I forget," said Susan, stopping at the door. "Professor Johnson wants to see you right away in his office. He was looking for you in the dining room."

After Susan had left, Laura wondered what Professor Johnson was so anxious to see her about. She hoped her work hadn't slipped in any way.

When she arrived at his small office, he was smoking a pipe and reading some papers. As he motioned her to come in and sit down he lowered his pipe and cleared his throat with a short cough.

"What I have to say won't take long," he began, readjusting himself in his chair behind a long desk. He coughed again. "I suppose you're wondering why I wanted to see you this . . . ah, early. It's not your work. You're doing fine. . . ." He hesitated a moment as he directed a curious gaze at her. He crossed a large leg over his knee and leaned back nervously in his chair. "Hmmm . . . how shall I put this? . . . Are you happy here, Laura?"

"Of course," Laura replied, adjusting herself in the small chair and now more puzzled than anxious. "This is what I wanted to do: to come here to study writing and work for you."

"Ah, yes," he said nervously. "And, uh, everything fine with Bill?"

Laura hesitated. "Of course."

"Good, good. Well, there's no sense in beating around the bush, is there? What I really wanted to question you about is your friendship with Mr. Tanner. Do you mind?" he asked, picking up his pipe to relight it.

Laura felt the blood rush to her face. Had someone seen her go into Jared's house?

"My friendship with, with . . . Mr. Tanner?"

"Yes," he said, puffing slowly on his pipe. "Of course, it's a good idea to mix socially with the faculty, that's part of your job, but Mr. Tanner is an unusual man, a little more than the usual teacher, but . . ."

Laura felt a mixture of incredulity and anger.

"But what?" she asked coldly.

"I'm sorry to have to say this," he continued. "You're a nice young woman, but Mr. Tanner is, well, obviously I have no jurisdiction over him—he's a guest lecturer, but I do have a responsibility for you. You're both my assistant and a student. Frankly, Mr. Tanner has the reputation of being a rake and I don't want any . . . unpleasantness for you. Do you follow me?"

Laura sat stiffly, trying to overcome a painful emotional turmoil. She finally succeeded in finding her tongue.

"I don't have a special friendship with Mr. Tanner," she said. "And I don't see how the institute has the right to concern itself if I do."

He ignored her statement. "You do see I'm saying this for your own good, don't you, Laura?" He tapped his pipe impatiently against his ashtray. "I mean, Bill . . ."

Laura rose to her feet. "I'm sorry you found it necessary to say anything to me. I think I'm capable of taking care of myself. Neither you nor the institute nor Bill need worry about me."

Professor Johnson stood up in his slow manner.

"We're guests of this village, Laura," he said, "and the Spanish people are very staid in ways. You're my administrative assistant, thus more than the ordinary tourist element in their midst. I trust you understand that—it's just a word to the wise."

"Thank you," Laura said as brusquely as she could.

Professor Johnson came around his desk and opened the door for her, his expression stern. "I'm sorry about this," he said.

Laura had no answer and fled to the safety of her room. Once inside she leaned back against the door a little dazed. To be told not to "get carried away" by Jared Tanner was mortifying. She was sure Professor Johnson was overstepping his bounds of authority. What had he been told and by whom? That she'd been seeing Jared on the sly? Students were always flocking around Jared, both in the classroom and in the café; she wasn't the only female around. Were there still rumors about their night on the mountain? Had someone seen her go into his house that evening?

His warning hurt. She felt she was being singled out. It was unfair. Professor Johnson was turning a deaf ear and a blind eye to dozens of blossoming student romances, but he didn't want his precious institute tinged with gossip about his assistant and his prized lecturer.

Laura was not going to be a mouse running madly for the nearest hole when someone scared her. She hated the thought that she was expected to watch her every movement, her every word, every glance. Whatever rumors were going around probably were not going to fade no matter what she did. In seven weeks Bill would be coming over for the Christmas holidays and her emotional life would become normal. All she had to do was play distant, lock up her heart, and wait. Jared had never made a move toward her in public nor was he likely to, even though he had asked her if she wanted him to court her openly. Her face heated remembering his whispered words to her. Had he meant what he said? He couldn't have. It was simply said in the heat of lust, a way to seduce her. And she had almost believed him—she'd wanted to believe him.

Finally she left to go and meet Susan's man in the café. Jared might be there at this hour but she was not going to let him or Professor Johnson run her life.

The café was quiet. Susan was sequestered with her friend in a corner and she waved as she saw Laura come in. Laura had been prepared to find a dashing philanderer on holiday from London, but seated beside Susan was a dignified man with glasses and sandy hair and a gentle smile—Bob Stewart. He got to his feet as Susan made introductions. His smile was kind and shy and he seemed genuinely pleased to meet Laura as Susan's friend. He was dressed in a quiet tan suit, neat with a tie and shirt. Susan was obviously proud to be next to him, and she prompted him to tell Laura about the hotel in Palma whose interior he was designing. It was an entirely new Susan who listened attentively to his diffident explanations of his work.

Laura looked up at the noisy entrance of a number of people from the restaurant next door. Relief must have shown on her face when she saw Jared was not among them.

"I thought I'd said something wrong for a moment," Bob said in his quiet manner. "You looked like you were about to see a ghost."

Laura smiled at him, apologizing for giving him a

turn, and then she made her excuses. She had been pleased to meet him and said so sincerely.

Susan beamed at her. "Thanks for coming. I'll see you tomorrow."

Another group of students and local residents were making their way through the door of the café as Laura tried to weave between them to make her exit. She was fighting through the throng when a hard hand pressed around her arm. Jared was beside her giving her a look of such intensity she thought his eyes would sear a path through her. "I need to talk to you," he said.

"I have nothing to say to you," she said in a throaty voice. "Let me go, please." At the look of distress on her face he let her go.

"Tomorrow," he said firmly. May came up beside him.

Flushing with anger, she shook her head no and left the scene.

Laura wondered what her response to Jared's pursuit should be. Should she totally avoid him? She couldn't cut her class indefinitely unless she decided to drop the course with him. That looked like her only alternative and yet it made her feel cowardly, as though she was avoiding a confrontation with the enemy. The real enemy was her traitorous heart.

That evening she went into Susan's room to praise her boyfriend.

"Bob's nice," Laura reported, smiling.

"That word! Sounds like my mother," said Susan, hands on hips.

"He is, Susan, and I have to admit I was surprised. I expected someone quite different."

Susan arched an eyebrow. "Someone as complicated as Jared?" She grinned mischievously, knowing the dart went home. "I've got a hunch about that man," Susan went on. "He's tired of his old life and is ready to settle down and I don't think he wants to settle with someone like May. He wants someone very special."

Laura felt tired, and turned to go back to her room. "I hope he finds her."

"Don't turn tail, Laura," Susan said thoughtfully. "He's only a man."

"That's something I won't forget," Laura replied, and left.

In the morning Laura asked Susan to turn in her latest assignment to Jared. It was her last class with him this week and for the next several days she would avoid him. She needed time.

"What do you want me to say to him?" Susan asked, her blue eyes sparkling with mischief.

"Nothing. Don't get fancy. Just turn in my paper with yours. He doesn't need a reason for my not being there and I doubt he'll expect any."

"Don't worry, I'll do it your way. But I warn you, men have a way of knowing what's in our devious minds anyway." She laughed and left.

Laura wrote a brief neutral letter to Bill and, when she had completed her work for Professor Johnson, walked up to the village post office to mail it. Seeing May Donnelly's white sports car parked outside, she hesitated and turned to leave. She couldn't be sure Jared wouldn't be inside, and she didn't feel like seeing May either.

"Oh, Laura, there you are." It was May's light

voice. Laura stopped and turned around, feeling something like a matador. "I've been meaning to see you," May went on, her smile not reaching her eyes. "I'm glad I ran into you like this. How are you?"

"I'm fine, May," Laura said, waiting warily.

"Sit down, won't you?" May said, as if she were in her own living room and not in the street outside the post office. May sat down on the stone wall along the narrow road and patted a place beside herself for Laura. "I don't think I need to tell you how surprised I was to see you at Jared's . . . Mr. Tanner's house the other night," May said without further introduction.

"I was invited," Laura replied.

"That's beside the point," May snapped. "Mr. Tanner has invited several students over for informal discussions."

Laura's heart contracted. May certainly knew the details of Jared's life. He had said the same thing to her.

"And do you interrogate all of them?" asked Laura.

"You're treading on the wrong ground if you think Mr. Tanner's any more interested in you than he is in his other students," continued May, ignoring her question. "In fact, he's tired of his lecturing; it takes too much of his time. He has other more important projects to attend to. He's just finished a script for a British television show, or didn't you know?"

"No, I didn't know," Laura admitted.

"No, of course not. Why should you know?" May tossed her blond head, giving Laura a triumphant look. "I've known Mr. Tanner for quite a time now," May continued in a purring voice. "I know the kind of life he leads. This sojourn of his is a sort of working vacation. When we leave here this will all become just a chapter in a book to him." She smoothed the skirt of her plaid wool dress with a long hand.

When we leave here: the words drummed in Laura's ears.

"Are you and Jared engaged?" Laura asked almost against her will.

"Oh, you can't be that innocent!" May said impatiently. "This is the twentieth century, Laura. Relationships don't turn on engagement rings anymore."

"No?" said Laura a fleeting thought of Bill registering.

"We haven't announced anything, but this is hardly the right place for it. There isn't anyone here to announce it to." May uncrossed her legs and stood up, giving Laura her chiseled smile. "Well," she went on. "I'm so glad I ran into you like this. I feel better now that we've had a little talk. I was sure we could reach an understanding."

Laura also stood up. "I'm not sure I understand totally, May," she said, "but I've got a clear impression that you're worried about something." Laura turned on her heel and went into the post office to mail her letters home. She heard May get into her car and drive away, and the tension left her shoulders.

For the first time in her twenty-one years Laura felt a wave of cynicism. May had given her warning. Surely if May knew Jared loved her she wouldn't have to be concerned about Laura. May obviously wasn't sure of Jared after all.

Chapter Seven

The encounter with Professor Johnson and May Donnelly had a perverse effect on Laura: she decided to stop avoiding Jared. Although she still felt that Jared was only pursuing her because of their strong physical attraction to each other and was determined not to be caught up in his charm or be foolish, she was *not* going to be a child and simply avoid him. If the whole world were saying "stay away from that man," the world was nevertheless helpless against the strength of her simple decision to stop resisting and let the chips fall where they may.

And so, after one of his classes she actually came up to his desk afterward to ask an innocuous question about a novel of Joseph Conrad's he had mentioned. She was pleased to see him look startled at her approach although he then talked with her easily.

At the café she forced herself to saunter over to say hello to him, even if he was with May. She was quite careful not to seem flirtatious but she refused any longer to flee and hide. Jared, while warm and polite, seemed to be watching this new development with amused irony but for a week made no further move to be alone with her.

Then one weekday afternoon she decided to take the bus to Soller, a large town ten miles north of Deyá, in order to buy a present for her father's birthday. She shopped for an hour and a half, finally settling on a leather belt for her father and finding an exquisite white lace mantilla for her mother.

When the shops closed at six she ate a ham and cheese *bocadillo* and *café con leche* in a café nestled against a cliff in the little ring-shaped port of Soller and then took the train back to the center of town. The last bus back to Deyá left at eight. As she was waiting a horn sounded and she turned and saw a familiar car. His elbow on the window, Jared was smiling at her.

"Can I give you a ride back to Deyá?" he asked.

"I'm taking the bus back, thanks," she answered quickly.

"Don't be silly," Jared said, throwing open the passenger door for her.

As she remained standing indecisively the cars behind Jared in the narrow street began honking their horns.

"Laura," Jared persisted. "You're holding up traffic."

Feeling a slight resentment at his bullying tactics, Laura gathered up her parcels and climbed into the car. As she pulled the door closed and settled in beside him she saw Jared smiling at her.

"Do you always commandeer people this way?" she asked.

"Only when I see the need. I learned long ago that if you want something, you have to reach out for it. Plums don't fall into your lap." He laughed softly. "If you don't mind being likened to a plum."

"A nut, maybe, to have allowed you to do this," she said.

He was driving up the winding road toward Deyá faster than Laura would have liked, but he was very much in command of the car.

"I'm nervous," she said, knowing that she really wasn't so concerned about the speed of the car as she was about Jared himself. She put a hand out in front of her against the dashboard. There was barely room for two cars and, with the darkness, Laura felt as though they were hurtling along an unknown and dangerous route.

He slowed down. "Your defenses are showing," he said.

"No, just my common sense," she answered.

Laura slanted a look at his profile, taking in the firm chin, the black hair falling forward over his brow, and felt the inevitable warmth flowing to her solar plexus.

As if challenging her thoughts, he asked, "Would you rather be with your fiancé?"

"Wouldn't you rather be with May?"

"Laura, why do you fight me so hard?"

"I'm not fighting you," she answered. "I only do battle when something is at stake."

"Like your virtue?" he said quietly.

"More than that. My destiny."

"You're overdramatizing," he said, removing his right arm from the steering wheel to drape it on the back of her seat. A sweet stab of desire pierced her.

He was so close. She fought the urge to lean back against his arm. When his fingers played lightly with her hair, a shiver of anticipation went through her, but she pulled her head away.

"Can you type for me?" he suddenly asked her.

Laura blinked at him. "What?"

"You know, on a typewriter. I need a typist for about two hours each day. I'll pay you well, if you'd like to help."

As the tension drained out of her Laura laughed. "You took me by surprise. I can't, Jared."

He put his hand on the back of her neck and softly caressed her. "Why not?" he asked. "Do you have too much work or are you uncertain about being too close to me?"

Again she pulled herself forward away from his touch. "There are others who would type for you at the institute. I can ask, if you like."

"No, I'll do my own asking. I would enjoy having you work with me." He brought his hand back to the wheel.

"It would be too—" She couldn't bring herself to say compromising. Didn't he know there was gossip about them?

"So, I'm cast forever in the role of devil or pirate, and no way out?" He teased, but his voice had an edge to it. "Is that the sword between us?"

She didn't understand him, and felt troubled. Jared gave her a quick glance.

"Maybe I like having you around," Jared persisted.

She felt warmed by his words but knew it was impossible. "It wouldn't work, Jared," she said. "I was called into my employer's office recently to receive an unofficial reprimand. He, well, he wanted to see me about you."

"What about me?" Jared's tone was sharp with annoyance.

"I won't repeat everything he said, but he thinks my seeing you might create a scandal. The institute's reputation could be damaged."

"Johnson said that to you?" His tone sounded incredulous. She could see his nostrils flare with anger as he thought about it for several long moments. "What else did he say?" he demanded next.

"Nothing. He was just warning me."

"The man is presumptuous. I can't tell you how angry I am."

"I think he was only trying to protect me."

"From the moral monster Jared Tanner?" he asked. She flushed in the darkness.

"And you agree with him, don't you?" he said flatly.

"No," she said. "Not really. I'm here with you."

"Only because I practically forced you to come with me." As he parked the car in front of his darkened house, Laura realized that they had driven past her *pensión*. Jared turned off the engine and remained, staring forward with his hands on the wheel. Laura was aware of an unresolved silence between them—the streetlight sculpting Jared's stern features with light and shadow. Finally, he turned to her.

"Laura," he said softly. "I still feel as I did a week ago when we were last alone. I want you. I want you to come with me into my house. I assure you this time we won't be interrupted."

"Jared, I can't come in," Laura said in a quiet voice.

Jared reached over and pulled her roughly to him.

"Because you don't want your feelings about me public, or because you don't trust me?"

Shaken, she put her hands up between them.

"I don't know," she said, feeling tears welling up in her eyes. "I don't know you." Even in the dark she could sense the storm in his face.

"I suppose I could try to change your mind again, but there isn't any point, is there?" he said, releasing her. "Inside you're still just tasting desire but not ready for the rest of it."

As she heard the condescension in his voice she felt a rush of anger. "I'm not afraid to love, Jared," she countered. "But I think you are."

Jared seemed to flinch at her words. "What do you mean?" he said.

"You may be an expert on physical desire," she continued, feeling a strange mixture of anger and pain, "but still be a dunce on other emotions."

Jared's eyes flashed and he started to respond but stopped himself, his face shredded by conflicting emotions.

"The student lecturing the teacher," he finally commented.

"Good night, Jared," she said softly, trying to fight back the tears she could feel welling up behind her eyes. She pulled away and slid over and opened the passenger door. One of her parcels tumbled to the floor and she had to retrieve it.

"I take it you don't want me to walk you home?" he asked sardonically.

She could feel the barriers rising between them but felt helpless at stopping them.

"No," she said, and she turned and began slowly to leave. As she walked away and the silence behind her lengthened, she felt her heart sinking with each step: He was letting her go.

The next morning when Laura entered Jared's classroom a few minutes late, a student was seated at his desk. To her total surprise Jared was not in the room.

"In Mr. Tanner's absence," the student was saying, "we're taking turns conducting the class. I got a note this morning asking me to be the first to read my story." He then launched into a dramatic reading.

Laura sat in a state of confusion. Jared had said nothing to her about going anyplace. When class ended she asked a classmate what had happened to him.

"He and Miss Donnelly left for London today. I guess he had some contract to take care of or something; in any case he won't be back until next week."

Laura was silent with shock. Turning quickly away before the student could read her expression, Laura gathered her papers and slowly pulled on her camel sweater and left as unobtrusively as she could.

Trying to pull herself together, she did a few ordinary things, checking her schedule of work for Professor Johnson and sorting the letters to be mailed. Still too upset to settle into her familiar typing and filing routine, she decided to post the mail first.

Walking to the post office, she felt dazed. She didn't

know what she had expected, but it wasn't this sudden slap in the face. What a fool she had been. There was no other word for it. He hadn't said a word to her about going to London . . . and with May.

Her anger with him making her fingers tremble, she stamped the neatly typed institute letters and gave them to the post mistress and picked up the mail. Sorting it through quickly, she saw a letter to her from Bill and felt a rush of relief. It was the lifeline she needed. However, she wanted privacy and a chance to collect herself before she could read it properly. Not wanting to go back to her room where she might have any number of people accosting her for their own legitimate needs or social reasons, she opted to take a long walk.

But before she could escape the village, Sheila came skipping up to her. She and Laura hadn't talked about her "problem" since she'd first raised it two weeks before.

"Hi, Laura," Sheila said, her bright eyes and cheerful face a distinct contrast to their meeting in Laura's room.

"Hello, Sheila," Laura said, stopping reluctantly. "How are you?"

"Oh, great. John Martin's taking me to hear a Spanish rock group in Palma tomorrow."

"That's wonderful . . . I take it that your problem . . ."

"Oh that," said Sheila with a superior shrug of her shoulders. "Jared was just a phase I was going through. As soon as I saw through him everything was fine."

"I'm glad," said Laura.

"At first I liked his sophistication, but then I realized that he's just old, you know? Miss Donnelly can have him. Judy!" In a burst of energy Sheila swept past Laura toward two students coming from the *pensión*.

Laura turned and mindlessly started walking toward the beach, then changed her mind. Memories of Jared would be there and that was the last thing she wanted now. She veered off, heading toward an ancient ruined tower on a promontory overlooking the Mediterranean that had been erected as a lookout for pirate ships long ago. She was determined to recover from the pain she was feeling.

There was a chill breeze as she walked across the terraces into a pine woods near the tower, but it was a clear sunny day and below her the water was a vivid green. Facing the sea, she sat on a boulder near the tower and read Bill's letter. It was a long one responding to the letter she had written filled with doubt and telling him of changes in herself. He had been distressed by it and unhappy that he couldn't be there to comfort and help her. He acknowledged that he had been through some "confusion and conflict" since their separation too, but felt he had now resolved it and loved her more than ever. Their separation had been a bad mistake, and they both had to be firm with themselves to hold their love together until they could reconfirm it when he visited over the Christmas holidays.

The letter was serious and thoughtful and seemed to imply that Bill might have been involved somehow with another woman but that he was over it and missed her and wanted to be back close to her. She read it three times.

As she stared down the cliff-edge toward the green water a hundred and fifty feet below she remembered the psychological cliff-edge she'd felt herself on with Jared during the time she'd been in his house. She'd been close then to ending her commitment to Bill and giving herself to Jared for what would inevitably have been a brief bittersweet fling. As she thought about it now she felt relief that she had stepped back from that precipice. No matter how strong her feelings, she was out of her element with Jared; she belonged with Bill.

She stood up. It was time to stop being weak. It was time to say a final and irrevocable "no" to her feelings for Jared, feelings which could only lead to a long fall. Bill was her "intended" and it was time to return to him in all ways.

As she stood there staring out across the sea she saw a sailboat on the horizon and imagined a full-sailed galleon pulling into the cove. She pictured the excitement in the village as the people rallied to defend themselves from the pirates.

Laura gave a shudder. But it wasn't from cold or fear; it was her involuntary image of Jared as a pirate. Would he have captured her? She almost said his name aloud, a longing filling her; but the deed was done: She had fought him off.

Slowly, not feeling the exhilaration she thought she should feel, she retraced her steps to the village.

Back at the *pensión* she busied herself doing the work Professor Johnson asked of her, glad to sink herself into it. She dreaded the day of Jared's return. She wouldn't know what her reaction would be until she saw him. The nights were the worst, when she turned out the lights and felt her own emptiness. She tried to think of Bill and her work, especially her writing, but it didn't work. During the day, Jared's class seemed sterile without his presence, just a room full of people talking aimlessly about writing. It was like a vacuum before a storm, the air around her impending, as if waiting to be filled.

Susan tried to penetrate through her moodiness, but she didn't feel like confiding in Susan. She couldn't bring herself to tell her either about what had transpired between herself and Jared or about her own feelings. She wanted to forget them. Susan, however, was quite able to put everything together without being told. And for some reason, unfathomable to Laura, she took Jared's side. Not that she didn't approve of Bill, but that she found Jared forgivable.

Maybe Susan liked him secretly or maybe she was just following her reporter's nose for the better story. Jared made good copy, Laura bitterly conceded. Pirates always made news.

Toward the end of the week Susan got a letter from her parents. "I'm going to London over the Christmas holidays," she announced. "My parents are going to meet me there. Some kind of convention—doctors' stuff."

"That's wonderful, Susan. You'll be able to introduce them to Bob there, won't you?"

"I guess so," Susan said, looking away.

"You don't sound very enthusiastic," Laura said, noting Susan's gloomy expression. "What's the matter?"

"Bob's leaving Sunday—I guess I told you," Susan replied. "But I didn't tell you we're splitting up."

"Oh, Susan, I'm sorry."

"Strange, isn't it. But we both began to realize that though we enjoyed being with each other, and respected each other, there was no . . . spark. He was the first man to treat me like a really mature woman and for a while I made that out to be more than it was." She sighed and then giggled. "He sure had me dreaming." She looked up at Laura wistfully. "But you know something? It's a consolation to know there are men around who can take me seriously—and some of them must have—pizzazz."

"Do you still see him?" Laura asked.

"Oh, yes, we're friends, but the heart's gone out of it. He's been good for me. Now I know what I want in a man: Someone more serious, who's sweet, and who likes me both for my zany side *and* my serious side."

"Your zany side?" said Laura, smiling. "Whatever can you be talking about?" They both laughed.

"What do you hear from Bill?" Susan asked next, unexpectedly.

Laura pushed her hair away from her face. "Oh, he's doing fine," she replied. "He's working in the emergency room this month."

"He's like Bob in some ways," mused Susan.

"Bill?" asked Laura, her eyes widening.

"I mean he's the serious, dependable type. Don't you think so?"

"You mean he's destined to be a good friend?" Laura asked ironically, smiling. Susan laughed.

"You said it, not me."

They were interrupted by a student coming in and

announcing that Laura had an overseas telephone call. Laura felt a jolt, afraid it might be Jared. She ran to take the call.

Laura's hands trembled as she picked up the receiver in the office.

"Hello?" she managed, her knees feeling weak.

"Well, hello to you too, how are you?" With a shock, Laura realized it was Bill, and couldn't answer.

"Hello, hello, are you there? Oh, no, I've got a bad connection," Bill said.

"Bill!"

"Laura, it's me. Who did you think it was? Where were you?"

"I . . . I was in my room. How . . . how are you?"

"I'm fine. It's great to hear your voice. Listen, honey, I'm coming over for Thanksgiving. Christmas isn't going to work out. I've already booked a flight. Can you meet me at the airport? I've got a lot to tell you and a special early Christmas present for you."

"Oh! . . . That's wonderful. Bill . . . I don't know what to say. You've taken me by surprise." Laura felt tears coming into her eyes.

"Honey, I know how you feel. It's been too long. Laura? Honey, listen carefully now. My flight is number 404 on Wednesday the twenty-fourth. I'll put it all down in a letter for you. I can't wait to see you. Everything's fine here. What have you been doing?"

"I can't wait to see you either, Bill. Everything's all right here too," she replied, hesitating unexpectedly over the words in a confusion of feelings.

Laura listened as Bill went on to tell her about people and places that seemed remote to her and answering his questions about her job with Professor Johnson. Then he stunned her.

"And honey," he said. "I think I want you to come back here to New York next semester. That last letter you wrote woke me up. This separation isn't working at all."

When she didn't reply, there was a brief silence.

"We can talk about it after I get there," Bill went on. "All I know is I miss you terribly and want you back here."

"I miss you too, Bill," Laura said quietly.

"Good-bye, honey. This call is costing a boodle, but it's worth it. See you soon."

"Yes, see you . . ." And he rang off.

Laura replaced the receiver and stood frozen a minute before slowly returning to her room. Susan was gone. Laura sat down stiffly on a hard wooden chair and found herself staring at the photo of Bill on her bureau. He was coming in ten days. He wanted her to leave Mallorca for good in only six weeks. He had a special gift for her. The pleasure and relief of talking with Bill was oddly mixed with a sorrow at thoughts of Jared and their failure. Part of her looked to Bill as a salvation from the powerful emotions stirred every time she saw or thought of Jared. Bill would steady her, remind her of her saner self. Bill would rekindle the warm feelings of closeness she had with him and make her forget the fires that raged with Jared. Bill was coming. She only hoped he arrived in time.

Chapter Eight

On Monday Jared was back. Laura went to his class feeling determined to be detached, so she wasn't prepared for the shock of seeing him again. He looked thinner, his face remote, tired. When he glanced at her she thought she saw a look of pain appear on his face. Yet as soon as he began the class the old commanding Jared reappeared. He told the class of his week in London visiting television studios and publishers and made it seem an insane and comic world of money-mad businessmen totally unrelated to the serious work they were doing in the class. When he'd finished and answered a few questions about his trip—again with satirical replies—he asked various students what they had read and discussed in class. After they'd told him he smiled.

"It sounds like all went quite well without your fearless leader," he commented. "My benevolent dictatorship seems to have fostered a healthy democracy. Nevertheless, I hope you'll let me resume my role." He smiled again and glanced at some notes. "I'd like to hear from someone who hasn't read his work in class before. Any volunteers?"

Laura's heart quickened. She was one of those who hadn't read anything in class, as he well knew. It hadn't been from shyness as much as from a desire not to have his attention on her while she read—a different kind of shyness.

"Laura," he said when no one volunteered. "That last paper you wrote is worth a read." His voice was dry as he made the statement. There was a moment of silence before she answered.

"I'm sorry," she said. "I didn't bring it with me."

He raised an eyebrow and seemed to hesitate.

"Would you excuse yourself, please, and go get it while Martha reads her story."

Laura reluctantly rose to retrieve it, but she wasn't sure she could bring herself to read it herself. As she went to her room she was again overwhelmed at a feeling of sadness at the ending of her life in Deyá, her life with Jared. When she began going through her manuscripts she made a quick decision: She would read the autobiographical story she had written about the relationship of a young woman with a famous and unscrupulous artist. In it she had consciously exaggerated the selfish and unprincipled characteristics of the artist in order to make the dilemma of the heroine with her powerful love the more dramatic. The feelings of the protagonist, however—the passion and the conflict—were her own. It was by far and away the most personal and emotional piece of writing she had ever done. She had never intended to turn it in, much less read it aloud in class. Yet she felt it was good. She'd already rewritten it three times while Jared was in London. It seemed to her a fitting epitaph for their failed relationship.

Martha had finished reading her paper when Laura returned. There was a brief discussion before Jared asked her if she was ready. From the neat pile of papers she placed on her desk Laura began reading with a clear, determined voice, a voice she kept carefully detached from the powerful emotions of the story. As she read she became aware of the silence in the classroom, of Jared's statuelike stillness fifteen feet in front of her. When she came to the page of the passionate love scene she hesitated but then went on undaunted. It was a long story and she realized dimly that the normal class time had probably elapsed, but Jared remained silent and there was no restlessness around her.

Finally she finished. Jared was leaning against the desk. He had been cupping his chin in a hand and he now let his arm fall slowly to his side. He was looking past her out the classroom window. He seemed disturbed, uncertain. He walked a few steps to the center of the room and turned to face the students, who had remained awesomely silent.

"Any comments?" Jared asked, his face once again under full control.

"Whew!" one of the male students said, and the tension in the room was released into several sighs and low nervous laughter. "No, I mean . . . it was really terrific."

Jared nodded absently and paced away to a corner before turning.

"Let's hope none of us meets that particular artist down a dark alley," he said, smiling and again there was laughter. Then he asked the class for their reactions to the character development and the tightness of the plot. The students who commented praised the story, especially the dialogue and interior monologues of the woman, and Laura sensed that the praise was honest rather than mere politeness. But then Jared, noting the time, told them the class was over.

"I'd like to see you a moment, Laura," he added.

Still riled up from reading her story she gathered up the pages and, as the others filed out, went up to Jared. Squaring her shoulders she looked up at him. He swept her briefly with his eyes, catching hers for an instant before she averted them. He let out a long sigh.

"Well, I think I'm lucky to have escaped an unauthorized biography, don't you?" he said teasingly.

She was glad to see his playfulness returning and winning out over the fatigue she felt she had noted earlier.

"I'm sure you've heard the old adage, 'If the shoe fits . . .'" she answered him.

He laughed.

"I'm not going to own up to being that man you described so graphically," he said, "no matter what you intended. Aside from that you handled your material well, very well. It was an extraordinarily fine story."

"Thanks."

Jared stood very still, observing her from a few feet away.

"I don't need thanks. I need a typist for two hours a day and I'd like you to do it for me."

"No . . . I can't."

"Why not?"

"Why don't you ask May? I'm sure she'd love to."

Jared walked over to the door of the room, closed it, and blocked the entrance with his body.

"There are several reasons why May can't do it. One is she doesn't type." His voice was low and deliberate. "The second is she's in London, and the third, most important reason is that I wouldn't want her to even if she could. I want you. Does that supply you with answers?"

Laura couldn't believe what she heard. It had never occurred to her that May hadn't returned from London. She must have had modeling business to take care of.

"It doesn't make any difference," Laura said finally. "You'll have to find someone else."

She could hear him give out a breath as if he was controlling his patience.

"I need someone I'm comfortable with, someone I can trust," he said quietly. "And someone who writes as well as you do. I'd like my typist to be able to pick up sloppy prose."

"You trust me?" she asked, thinking of her story.

"Yes."

"You're forgetting Professor Johnson's concern about my reputation," she said.

"I saw him this morning before class. I doubt he'll bother you again."

"What did you say to him?" she asked, a worried frown on her face.

"Nothing he'll repeat, so don't let it concern you. I know you need some extra cash, so I hope you won't continue stubbornly turning me down."

Laura hesitated, wanting to, but holding back.

"I can't," she said after a pause. "Bill is flying over

next week for Thanksgiving and . . . it wouldn't be right."

"Your fiancé is coming to Deyá?" Jared asked, his mouth tightening for a second in irritation.

"He's not really my . . . yes," she concluded.

"It doesn't make any difference. If it's my presence that's worrying you, you can rest easy. I'll guarantee I won't be there. There will be just you, the typewriter, and my work. Is that fair? I'll even commit myself on paper, if you like."

"There's no need for that." Laura sat down to consider his offer. "Are you willing to promise me something, a condition?" she asked him.

"What's that?" he asked, putting his hands in his pockets and leaning back against the door.

"Hand's off." She looked at him evenly.

She saw the faint compression of his lips.

"You?" he finished for her.

"Yes," she nodded.

"Agreed," he said without hesitation.

Her eyebrows raised skeptically. "I mean it, Jared," she said softly. "It's not fair to Bill and I don't trust you."

"You've made that clear any number of times. What makes you think you're irresistible?" he asked, throwing her a taunting smile.

Laura wished she had something in her hands that she could throw; then she was glad that she hadn't. He might deserve it. On the other hand, it wasn't the picture of aloofness she wanted to give him. Her eyes, however, betrayed her temper. He stood up and put a hand on the door.

"Come over today at five. I have a deadline and I'm

falling behind. Regardless of what you may think, I do need your skills and your help." He left before she had time to argue any further.

Laura knocked on his door at five fifteen trying to control her feelings. Jared opened the door, standing there a moment in a white shirt with rolled up sleeves and jeans. He smiled down at her, his eyes running over her quickly. The old feeling swept over her, and Laura grimaced as she fought it. He was too potent, like champagne, and the promise of a heartache the next day bubbled in the air.

"Come in, I've got it all ready for you." He let her pass through, the thud of the closing door sounding somewhat ominous. He had built a fire and the room was cozily warm. The typewriter was sitting on the desk, neat piles of papers around it.

"Sit down," he said quietly. She took off her thick camel sweater and sat at the desk, awareness of him in every nerve.

"I need a perfect copy. It shouldn't be too much trouble," he said, as he indicated the papers to be typed. He explained in detail what he wanted her to do. She was conscious of a sweet pain as his bare browned arms arched near her and his hands pointed to problems she might encounter.

"If you have any questions, I'll be upstairs," he said, coolly withdrawing.

Laura looked up at him. "I thought you weren't going to be here?" She pushed her long hair back.

Jared paused at the stairway. "Where did you expect me to go?"

She searched his face. She had supposed he would go to the café. She hadn't really thought about it clearly.

"I think we can handle this impersonally, don't you?" His face was set impassively.

She nodded and he ascended the stairs.

Alone in the room she yanked her attention to the work she had agreed to do. She took some deep breaths to control her runaway senses, and began.

Jared's words were like the living man, controlled, yet forceful. She marveled at his ability to weave a spell, becoming engrossed in the story and typing the pages perfectly. Only once did she have to call him to decipher a word she couldn't read. He came down and briefly glanced at the word. In a distant voice he told her what it was and retreated without further comment.

An hour later he came down and told her casually that it was time for her to leave.

"I'll just finish this page," she said, flicking him a glance.

"All right," he said after a moment's hesitation and stood by the fire while she finished and took it out of the typewriter.

"Do you want to be paid each day or do you want to wait until you've finished? I can pay eight dollars an hour." Her eyes widened. It was generous. She wanted to tell him it was too much, but didn't, the discussion embarrassing her.

Laura drew on her sweater. "When I'm finished, I guess," she said, feeling awkward about being paid by him.

"I'll see you tomorrow then," he said without emotion and crossed to open the door for her.

"Good night, Laura." He held the door open for her.

Laura was dazed. She had been prepared for some attempt on his part to make this arrangement more intimate. His composure and distance at all times during the day took her by surprise.

"Good night," she said, hesitating to add his name. She was being dismissed like an employee.

Laura descended the terrace stairs and walked back to the *pensión* in the darkening day. He had said he would keep it impersonal, but she hadn't believed him. Now that it was happening as she had asked, she felt adrift, a floating log on a river. She smiled at herself: She obviously had unconsciously wanted him to try to seduce her again. What a hypocrite she was!

The attitude of some of the students toward her job didn't help. She told them that she needed the money the job was providing—which was absolutely true. Although Susan said nothing to her, she did comment that some of the girls had made catty remarks.

"With Bill coming," Laura had responded angrily, "I wouldn't be typing for Jared unless it were just a business relationship."

And that's actually all it was. The first few days of her working for him were as if she had never been in his arms and he had never shown such desire for her. She was convinced now that it hadn't meant anything to him. His indifference made it easier for her to be cool and distant, but the pain she had tried to bury when he had so precipitously gone to London with

May and when Bill's letter and phone call had made her recommit herself to Bill kept resurfacing sometimes in the form of aches or flashes of desire. Even in his remoteness and with her desire to kill her feelings she was drawn to him, his proximity still like oxygen.

When she arrived at Jared's house for a fourth day of work he asked her to drive his car to Palma while he drove May's white Porsche. He had greeted her at the door dressed to go and keys in hand, as if her refusal wasn't possible. "Typical," she thought. He was wearing his usual at-home jeans, but with a neat tan shirt and western style boots, his brown suede jacket slung over a shoulder. He looked like a poster ad for an American cigarette, she thought. Her eyes took in his handsome figure while he bent to dampen the fire in the grate.

"May's not coming back and wants her car shipped to America. I have to get it down to the docks. You drive, don't you?" he asked, straightening from his task.

"Of course," she answered him.

"Let's get going then. This may take some time."

He gave her instructions on the use of his car, putting the keys in the ignition himself, and told her to follow him closely.

Laura's driving skills were tested on the way down to Palma, her heart racing around the curves on the narrow winding road, trying to follow Jared's trail. He would occasionally disappear around a curve and had to slow down for her to catch up.

It was late before he finally got all the business details finished at the customs office. After they had emerged from the waterfront office and climbed into Jared's own car, he proposed they eat out, as she would have missed dinner at the *pensión* by the time they got back.

He drove to La Casa Verde, one of the best restaurants in Palma, and opened the door of the car for her. He didn't take her arm or offer his hand to help her out. He hadn't touched her since his return from London. Laura realized she wanted at least a simple gesture from him, one that would acknowledge her. Although it was madness she knew she wanted his touch.

He ordered a scotch for himself and a bottle of sparkling wine for dinner, and then, without asking her what she would like to eat, he had a long conversation with the waiter. In the end he ordered *gambas a la plancha*, shrimp broiled with a wonderful concoction of spices and garlic, and a rich fish stew with *marisco* and white fish. Then he began drinking his scotch, one hand resting on the table. An urge to reach over and touch his hand leapt through her, remembering their magic, and angrily she suppressed it.

"Hungry?" he asked her, his eyes cool as they regarded her.

"Starved," she answered, a trace of her irritation in her voice.

A brief light flickered across his features, a smile barely touching his lips, before he took another drink from his glass and looked away, his eyes coming to rest on a young woman at another table. Laura followed his gaze briefly to a beautiful dark-haired woman in animated conversation with her companions. She felt a stab of jealousy that was only relieved when the wine arrived. It was pale and bubbly, like champagne, and she drank deeply.

"Tell me about your first book. Was it easy to get it published?" she asked softly as she played with her wine glass. She wanted to break his icy indifference.

"Making polite conversation, Laura?" he asked.

She looked away from the sharp coolness of his eyes.

"No," she said when she had recovered from his remark. "I'm interested."

His eyes assessed her briefly, resting on her lips a moment. He shrugged and began telling her how he had gotten a lot of encouragement while young and then, on his own, had failed many times before finally getting a break. From then on it was hard work, but most everything he had written was published. As he spoke—with an almost insultingly impersonal approach to his story—his eyes went again to the dark-haired beauty at the table a few yards from theirs, and she saw him acknowledge her with his eyes when she smiled his way.

He looked up as the waiter arrived with their dinner and his face became again impassive. Wondering whether Jared was trying to make her jealous or was genuinely indifferent to her, Laura took another gulp of her wine. She looked blankly at the steaming *gambas* as he dished out a portion for her. When her plate was full Laura toyed with her food, eating a little of the delicately scented saffron rice. They ate in a silence that became increasingly painful to her.

Then the dark-haired woman was leaving. As she slowly passed by their table, her eyes fixed on Jared, she stopped briefly to comment on the dish they were eating. Jared looked up at her with a smile and answered in polite Spanish, agreeing with her. With a flagrant fluttering of long lashes the woman left.

"I'm cramping your style," Laura said when the woman had gone.

"No more than I will cramp yours with Bill," he said, his voice ironic. Laura put her fork down and looked away, staring at nothing in particular. "Finish your dinner," Jared suggested quietly.

Laura turned back slowly and resumed eating. His voice acquired a softer note as he asked her about her opinions of the work she was typing for him. The tension between them gradually faded as she saw he was genuinely interested in what she thought. She was hesitant at first, but his questions encouraged her, making her feel she had something valuable to say.

"What I like about both this book and *Days of Gold* is the way your characters don't always act predictably," she said. "Just when I think I know what's going to happen, a character does something I hadn't expected, yet is still consistent with what we know of him."

"You like unpredictability?" he asked, smiling at her and setting down his fork as he finished his meal.

"In fiction, anyway," she replied. "I'm not so certain about whether I like it in life."

"You're right," he said. "Unpredictability in life can be rather inconvenient. Especially in a woman," he added.

"A woman!" Laura shot back. "You should talk."

"I never know whether you're a talented innocent or a cunning witch," Jared went on, ignoring her barb.

"I'm not a cunning witch," Laura said, pushing her plate away from her. "Just an ordinary innocent."

"If you're innocent," Jared countered, laughing, "Lord protect the male population when you finally become crafty."

She smiled.

"Why didn't you offer me a brandy too?" she asked as he took a sip from the cognac he had just been served.

"Forgive me. I'll order one if you like, but I thought you'd had quite enough spirits already. I wouldn't want to be accused of abusing your innocence," he grinned. "Or maybe I'm just too cheap. Take your choice."

"I don't think you're cheap, if what you're paying me for my typing is any indication." Silently she agreed with his evaluation of her wine drinking but still didn't like his deciding for her.

"Don't be too sure I won't take this dinner out of your salary."

She looked at him, wondering if he was going to do just that. She was on the point of saying that would be fine with her when he interrupted.

"I'm teasing you," he went on. "You should have been an actress, Laura. You're able to communicate such precise emotions with just your face and eyes. That ability to express emotion easily is a useful tool in an actress, just as being able to disguise emotions is in real life." He finished his drink and called for the waiter.

* * *

Later, driving home, he asked her if she could make up today's typing loss by extending her time tomorrow.

"I think so," she said without hesitation.

"I'm not interfering with your own work, am I?" he asked.

"No," she replied. "In fact, I'm sure that dealing closely with your writing will help my own."

Jared then began questioning her specifically about certain passages she had typed. She answered him honestly, telling him she had been fascinated as the story unfolded, but did feel that his character Jack was in one passage chauvinistic in a way that was at variance with his other actions, which were idealistic, almost heroic.

"I'm afraid such inconsistent characters actually exist," he responded, sounding amused. "Although you may be right that his action doesn't work in that particular scene."

"Do you want the character to be realistic?" she asked, frowning at him.

"Yes and no," he replied. "I want to highlight what's already in life, compressing time. Authors like me omit the ordinary, like long hours of writing or typing, or taking a walk nowhere in particular, or making long languorous love to his woman." His voice had been without inflection, but Laura felt a rush go through her at his phrase "long languorous love" and felt her cheeks heighten with color.

"Nothing personal," he added, watching her with a smile.

He drove the last rise in the road into the village,

and pulled up in front of the *pensión*. When he reached across her to open the door, the fleeting touch stirred her, and she quickly got out of the car.

"Good night, Laura," he said, his face turned to her in the dark, but his voice was merely polite.

Jared had a pile of work for her the next day. She was getting used to his cool voice explaining what she had to do. He came down later in the morning to make coffee for himself, and he gave her a cup.

"Can you type a letter or two for me?" he asked, laying them on the desk.

"I see," she said. "Pretty soon you'll be asking me to do your laundry." She smiled up at him and picked up her cup of coffee.

"I told you I had a lot of work," he said as he stirred the fire into life and added a log.

"Is it always like this?" she asked.

"When I have a deadline, yes. And come to think of it, even when I don't."

Laura wondered how he fitted his classes into his schedule. It was clear the life of a professional writer wasn't quite what the mass media made it seem.

"Maybe acting would be easier," she said dreamily.

Jared laughed. The sound was balm to her ears. She had forgotten, in their tension, how easily he laughed.

"I'm going to put a hamburger on to cook," he said. "Can I make one for you?"

"It looks like I'm going to be here awhile," she said. "You might as well." When she smiled at him he smiled back, his eyes capturing hers before he left for the kitchen. Laura bent to her typing, trying to get at least one of his letters done before her hamburger arrived.

Ten minutes later he put plates down in front of the fire and called her over.

"Just a minute," she said, typing carefully.

"Tired?" he asked when she had finished and came over to join him.

"I'm okay," she said, seating herself on a cushion and resting back against the wall. "But I appreciate the lunch." As she ate her hamburger she realized there was an ease between them that hadn't been there on the other days. She didn't know what it was, or why, but was glad.

"Do you want the day off tomorrow?" he asked her. He was sitting cross-legged in front of the fire. Red and yellow lights played across his dark features.

"Why?" she asked, puzzled.

"Your Bill is arriving. Or had you forgotten?"

She felt a stab of guilt that at times she had forgotten.

"Not until the afternoon," she said. She got up and took their plates into the kitchen, leaving him staring into the fire. In a few minutes he followed her, appearing in the kitchen doorway.

"Leave those for Francisca," he said to her as he watched her scrape the plates into a compost bucket and run hot water into the dishpan. "She'll be in tomorrow."

"It'll only take a minute," she said, turning to the sink and beginning to wash their few plates and cups.

"Better be careful," he said, smiling at her. "I've also got plenty of dirty laundry."

"I'm doing the dishes because I want to," she

replied, laughing. "If you ordered me to do them I'd go back to my typing."

"You try me sometimes," he said, shaking his head as he leaned against the doorframe.

"Good," she retorted teasingly.

He laughed and she saw a fleeting look on his face that made her hands tremble slightly as she washed the last cup and set it to drain beside the sink. As she finished he turned and left, calling out to her as he retreated up the stairway.

"Just do ten more pages and then get on home," he said. "Forget the other letter. I'll type it myself."

She returned to her typing, concentrating so that she could get the letter done before he came down again. She was typing the last words as he came down and put an envelope down beside her on the desk. She felt awkward when she realized what was in it.

"Don't look like that—you earned it," he said.

"Thank you," Laura said and picked up her sweater and headed slowly for the door.

"Wait a minute." He went back for the envelope and handed it to her.

Laura was embarrassed that she had forgotten and caused him to retrieve it. She took the envelope.

Jared moved to the door to open it for her.

"You're acting as if taking money from me were a sin," he said. "You've nothing to feel guilty about."

"I know," said Laura. "I don't know why it makes me feel funny."

"It's Bill's arrival," Jared said quietly.

She found it difficult to return his gaze. "I suppose so."

"Does he . . . appreciate you?" Jared asked softly.

"What . . . what do you mean?" she asked, aware of his eyes boring into her with that intense look she found unnerving.

"What a good typist you are," he said, smiling with sudden amusement. He opened the door for her. "What else could I mean?"

Laura slanted him a look beneath half-lowered lashes and then walked down the steps toward the *pensión*. What else *did* he mean?

Chapter Nine

Bill Lawrence made his way through customs at the airport and walked toward Laura with a big grin. His thick very curly brown hair haloed his face and he had grown a stylish mustache since she had last seen him. He was lugging a heavy brown leather suitcase and a plastic briefcase, containing, she guessed, medical books. He would fill his days and nights with activity. His blue suit coat was open and his red-striped tie loose. As she watched him approach Laura was aware that running through her general excitement was a thread of fear: he seemed something of a stranger to her.

"What a place!" he exclaimed to her as he gave her a bear hug and a brief kiss. "Just what I needed after slaving away at Brookhaven General for three months." He grinned down at her, squeezing her arms, and then began an inventory of the things he hoped they could do during his four-day visit. Somehow he had expected bullfights and grand cathedrals and museums, and as they made their way out of the terminal toward the car Laura had borrowed from Eric Tabor, he seemed slightly put off to hear that

Mallorca was more sedate and less spectacular than mainland Spain in tourist attractions.

"My flight was a bargain though," he continued as they began their drive up to Deyá. "And I knew you'd find me some reasonable accommodations. You did, didn't you?"

Laura reassured him that the Villa Rojo where she had found him a room was everything he could hope for: inexpensive, clean, and with a lovely view overlooking the village.

"That's my girl," he said approvingly. "What activities have you planned for us?"

"We're invited to Thanksgiving dinner tomorrow afternoon at Professor Johnson's," Laura answered, coming up with the only concrete plan she had made for them.

"That's nice. I'd like to meet him and his wife again, and some of your new colleagues."

The rest of the trip to Deyá was taken up with talk of Bill's work in the hospital and his meeting and liking a certain old Dr. Jones whose practice he was thinking of taking over when the old man reached retirement in a couple of years.

"He wants me to move in when my internship is finished," Bill concluded. "It might be good but I'm still kind of interested in doing a year of research at the lab. That might mean you'd have to support me an extra year, so I'll have to think about his offer some more. What do you think?"

Laura found she couldn't offer an opinion: She was still having trouble getting back into synchronization with Bill and all her old life.

"I think you should do what you think is best for

your career," she said after a long pause. "What you want to do most."

"That's great, honey. I knew you'd see it that way." He gave her a big smile.

Her smile back was strained.

Bill had been so wrapped up in the discussion of his career that he had barely noticed the spectacular scenery on the road up from Palma, but as they neared the village of Deyá he finally exclaimed at the "great mountains." As they slowed to enter Deyá he reached over and squeezed her thigh.

"It's good to see you again," he said, smiling happily.

"You too," she said, smiling, but noted how unmoved she was by his hand on her.

She left Bill at the *Villa Rojo* to shower and rest until they would meet again in an hour for an early dinner.

Returning alone to her own room, Laura was agitated. Although she had enjoyed being with Bill again, had felt a rush of warmth at first seeing him, all through the hour and a half they'd been together she had felt some part of herself holding back. She was angry with herself. Why couldn't she let herself go? And hanging over all her pleasure and interest at being with him was a cloud of sadness she couldn't account for. She assumed it must be related to her decision to give up Jared, and she was disturbed that her decision to recommit herself to Bill hadn't totally squashed those feelings.

She dressed carefully for dinner in a favorite gray wool skirt and red silk blouse that plunged in a low vee and wrapped around her waist. She added a long string of mock pearls knotted at the vee, and red sandals.

When Bill arrived in a navy jacket and white turtleneck he smiled and gave her a gentle kiss. He told her she looked and smelled good and asked her what perfume she was wearing.

Laura took him to the crowded, centrally located restaurant, knowing that Jared never went there anymore. He preferred quiet out-of-the-way restaurants or eating at his house. She smiled at a few friends as they entered, she introduced Bill to Eric Tabor, and then they were alone.

Bill seemed fatigued at first, but after a couple of glasses of wine he loosened up and launched into amusing reminiscences of some of their old times together back on Long Island, and they were both able to laugh. They had known each other since she was twelve years old, and although they hadn't really begun dating each other until a little over a year before, they shared a lot of memories.

It was after nine o'clock when they finally left the restaurant and began to amble up the little hill toward Bill's *pensión*. Laura was feeling a little sluggish from the wine and abundant food and as they slowly climbed she felt again a wave of sadness.

"Is there someplace we can go that's not so public?" Bill asked her with a smile as they neared the *pensión*. "Maybe the *señora* wouldn't mind your coming up to my room?" he added hopefully.

"I think she would. Deyá is a very tightly knit village. It's just not done," Laura replied, hoping her reluctance to be alone with him wasn't too noticeable.

As they stopped outside Bill took her in his arms.

"That doesn't give us a great deal of privacy then."

". . . Only the darkness," she said after a long hesitation.

Bill slowly lowered his face to hers and gave her a long kiss, warm and tender, but when he tried to deepen it and prolong it further, Laura found herself drawing back. Still holding her close, Bill looked puzzled.

"Hey, lady," he said. "I'm your boyfriend, remember?"

"I'm sorry. I feel a little awkward for some reason."

"Don't I know it," Bill said, relaxing a little. "So do I. Separation may make the heart grow fonder, but it's a real pain in every other way."

"I . . . Bill," Laura began, wanting to share with him some of the strange feelings she'd been having and some of the reasons for them. "I have something I want to talk to you about. It seems . . ."

"Laura," he interrupted firmly. "There's nothing you have to say. Your flying off to Mallorca was a mistake for us. I realized that from your last couple of letters. You feel a little estranged from me, right?"

Laura gently freed herself from his arms and moved slightly away from him.

"Yes, that's true," she said. "I . . ."

"It's only natural," Bill went on. "We haven't seen each other in almost three months. It's been too long." He came up behind her and put his hands around her waist. "In fact, honey, it's no good your being here. I want you to come back as soon as this semester is over."

She stiffened in his arms.

"Next semester?"

"Right. Take that job as medical secretary and be with me right at the hospital. We're wasting time being separated like this."

"It's awfully sudden," she said after a pause.

"Do you want us to be together or not?" he said, turning her around to face him.

". . . Of course, Bill . . ."

"I know it's sudden, but we're more important than anything else and I'm missing you too much. It's even affecting my work!" He laughed nervously.

She again released herself from his embrace and turned away from him in the darkness.

"I'd like to think some more about that one," she said. "You've only been here a few hours."

"It's like meeting all over again, isn't it?"

"I'm sorry . . ."

"We're both tired . . . jet lag . . . excitement," he said. "Maybe we'd better call it a night." From behind her he brought his face down and pressed his cheek against hers, his arms squeezing her waist. "Good night, my beautiful Laura," he whispered. "Don't worry, tomorrow we'll be as good as new . . ."

Feeling a rush of affection for him she turned in his arms and raised her face to be kissed. But as he kissed her and they embraced she had the eerie sensation of being detached, as if she were three feet above them looking down and merely observing.

"Good night, Bill," she said when he ended their kiss, and she gently freed herself from his arms and walked slowly away.

* * *

At noon the next day, after a pleasant morning hike with Bill among the olive groves, Laura dressed for the Thanksgiving celebration at the Johnson's. She chose her most sedate afternoon outfit: a simple wine-colored light-wool dress with a circular skirt and fitted waistline. Except for a bracelet Bill had once given her, she wore no jewelry. She was feeling peculiarly restrained at the prospect of Bill and Jared possibly meeting at the Johnson's.

Professor Johnson himself greeted them at the door of his attractive stone house on the hillside overlooking the village. Laura felt relieved that Jared wasn't among the guests, which included Maria and Eric Tabor, Elena Marvin, and the Spanish teacher, Jorge Miguelo.

Bill was introduced by Professor Johnson to everyone as "Laura's fiancé" and each time Laura felt the same nagging sadness. Bill himself mixed easily with all the guests, surprising Laura by briefly discussing the poetry of T. S. Eliot with Elena Marvin and Professor Johnson. Eric and Maria were their usual ebullient selves telling Bill they'd like to hear about his impressions of Deyá before he left, and Bill told them he "already liked it very much. It's so different."

They were sitting and drinking on the lovely stone patio outside the house, the fall sun slanting in over the mountain and through the leaves of the olive trees with brilliant light. It was warm enough to be comfortable, and as no one seemed to be making much of her or Bill, Laura, seated back in a lawn chair, began to relax. When Bill began talking to Professor Johnson and the Spanish teacher about diseases peculiar to the Mediterranean, she let her mind wander. Glad that

Bill fit in, she sipped at her drink and after awhile glanced contentedly down toward the village, but then sat up with a start. Making his way up the path toward the house was Jared. The sight of his long determined strides quickened her heartbeat. He was alone, dressed casually in a black sweater over neat gray trousers, a hand hooking a gray jacket over a shoulder.

"Isn't that right, honey?" Bill said from beside her.

"What? . . . I'm sorry, I didn't catch that last comment," she said, flushing.

"I was telling Professor Johnson that one of my purposes in coming here is to get you to return to the States after the first semester."

"Oh . . ." said Laura dazedly, aware that Professor Johnson and his wife were staring at her.

"Laura, you didn't warn me," Professor Johnson said, watching her carefully as he puffed on his pipe, a look of annoyance crossing his face.

"I . . . we . . . haven't definitely decided," Laura began, aware as she spoke of Jared heading toward her like an avalanche approaching a skier.

"I found I missed her much more than I thought I would," Bill went on jauntily. "Cadavers and throat cultures aren't as good company as they're cracked up to be."

"I've heard such good things about your writing, Laura," Mrs. Johnson said. "Does that mean you're giving it up?"

"When I finish my year-and-a half of internship, she can return to it," Bill interjected defensively.

Laura was too distracted to concentrate on what they were saying and didn't reply.

When Jared emerged onto the patio, Laura stiffened and took a large swallow from her glass.

Professor Johnson rose to greet him and in a few moments Jared was standing in front of them.

"I've met everyone else," she heard Jared say. "You must be the young intern who's come to cure Laura of her ills." She saw his dark eyes flash.

Bill stood up and shook hands.

"Bill Lawrence," he said with a relaxed smile. "And you must be the writer Jared Tanner. I haven't read any of your books, I'm afraid, but I've heard they're very good."

"I've been very lucky," Jared rejoined. "Are you having a nice visit?"

"Marvelous," Bill answered. As both men took seats, Professor Johnson handed Jared a scotch and water. "However, I've only been here a day. What do you suggest Laura and I do while I'm here?"

Jared laughed and Laura's hand tightened involuntarily around her glass.

"I'd rather not answer that question," he said, his eyes narrowing as he held his gaze on Bill. "But I think it might involve your taking a long trip."

"Really," said Bill, missing the hidden message. "We haven't gone more than a few hundred feet outside the village so far."

Laura felt an urge to throw the contents of her glass at Jared.

"And how are you, Laura?" Jared asked unexpectedly, pinning her with his eyes.

"Fine," she answered tightly, not looking at him.

"Cured of your disease?" he asked. Jared said the

word disease so it just managed to sound like "disease."

She slowly raised her eyes to his, aware they must show the anger she was feeling. She didn't reply.

"Disease?" Bill echoed. "Have you been sick, honey? You didn't tell me."

"It was nothing," she said slowly. "As soon as you arrived I began to be cured."

"You seem fine to me," Bill said. "I think you've been a little more subdued than I remember. Maybe you're anemic. Changes in climate and eating can do that to you."

Jared laughed.

"No," he said wryly. "Whatever ailed or ails Laura it isn't anemia."

The Johnsons' Mallorquin cook saved the day by announcing that dinner was served.

As she and Bill made their way into the house to the dining room Laura was aware of Jared close behind them. Mrs. Johnson was busily telling everyone where they should sit: Bill was on Professor Johnson's right, Laura opposite Bill to the Professor's left, and alternate male-female down to Mrs. Johnson at the other end of the table. Jared was to be at the opposite end of the table, but as Laura was breathing a sigh of relief at his distance he casually suggested to Jorge Miguelo that they change places so that Jorge could be next to Elena Marvin, whom Jorge was courting, and Jared stood triumphantly behind the chair next to Laura.

"Lovely afternoon," he said to her teasingly, aware of her discomfort.

The dining room was filled with ornate Spanish furniture, dark wood, and richly textured fabric on the beautifully carved chairs, and it produced initially a somewhat formal atmosphere. When the turkey had been carved and served and the champagne poured, Professor Johnson rose to propose a toast.

"To all present for a happy Thanksgiving," he said, raising his glass with a happy grin. "May you have full stomachs and plenty of Alka-Seltzer."

Everyone laughed and raised their glasses to drink the champagne. As Laura sipped from her goblet she became aware of Jared's thigh touching hers and his arm hot against her shoulder. She was sure he knew he was touching her and was making a point of doing so.

"I'd like to add to that one," Jared said raising his goblet on high, his deep voice commanding attention.

"To love. May we all find it and, more importantly, recognize it when we do."

There was a brief awkward silence and then a loud, "Hear, hear," from Eric Tabor and another raising of glasses. Laura sensed that Jared, beside her, had been looking at her during his toast, but she kept her eyes on her goblet.

The champagne and later wine flowed freely throughout the long meal, which Laura endured as a trial. The conversation flowed freely too, moving from Mallorca to the U. S., from medicine to literature, from teaching to doctoring. Throughout, Bill seemed relaxed and happy, a little high on the wine, and completely oblivious of anything special about Jared or his behavior. Laura was aware of every nuance of Jared and his actions. She sensed that as the meal progressed he had become calm, seeming to be concentrating on examining Bill, listening to him, watching as he and Laura interacted. But at the end of the dinner when they were all sitting around the living room, the setting sun making an orange pattern on the white living room wall, most of the guests replete or slightly drunk, the conversation took a turn that again seemed to rouse Jared.

"I'm afraid we may be losing Laura," Professor Johnson said with exaggerated casualness to Jared. "It looks like she'll be resigning as my assistant and returning to the U. S. in a month."

"Oh?" said Jared, meeting Professor Johnson's inquisitive gaze with studied coolness. He turned to Laura.

"The pace of life here too fast for you?"

She ignored his jab.

"Bill would like me to return," she said simply; her hand moved in a gesture of resignation.

"I don't blame him," Jared said, and turning to Bill, he added: "Laura's the sort of woman who has to be kept on a tight rein. She has a wild side to her that has to be checked."

"It's not that," said Bill. "It's just that I miss her and she can earn more money back in the States."

"Right," Jared said, his eyes glittering. "She's had her chance at writing and it's time for her to settle down."

"I wouldn't go that far," said Bill, shifting on his feet. "I hope she'll continue to do some writing. She won a prize once at Darrow."

Laura kept her head bent and turned the cut glass she held in her hand as if it were fascinating, annoyance with the conversation prickling down her spine.

"Have you read what she's written since she's been here?" Jared asked.

"Well, no," said Bill. "We haven't had the time yet. I guess you've been one of her teachers. Is it good?"

The exchange forced home that Bill hadn't even asked Laura about her work since she'd been here, and she couldn't help but feel that that had been exactly Jared's intention.

"Excellent. She wrote one story about a young woman and an artist, which is brilliant. It has everything going for it . . . except the truth." Jared's eyes pierced Laura.

"Is that right?" said Bill, his voice losing some of its early lightness. "I'd like to read it."

"There's no hurry," said Jared, still watching Laura even as he addressed his words to Bill. "You'll have plenty of time back in the States. It'll probably be the last story Laura ever writes."

"While you're here," Eric Tabor said to Bill loudly, "you should do some hiking above the village. There are some marvelous views."

"Oh, yes," said Jared, eyes gleaming. "You should climb the mountain. If you're lucky, miraculous things can happen up there."

"Really?" said Bill politely, now aware that Jared was baiting him for some reason.

"Oh, yes, a climb like the last one I had can change a man's life."

A tense hush settled over the room and Laura felt everyone looking at her. She knew that Bill must be confused by Jared's peculiar high energy and vague allusions.

"Jared has a vivid imagination." She smiled nervously at Bill.

"Have you been up?" Bill asked her.

"Yes," she said, refusing to elaborate, a flush pinking her cheeks.

"How was it?"

Professor Johnson began a violent coughing fit, and his wife began slapping him on the back.

"Laura got lost," Jared said affably. "Does she often get lost with you, Bill?"

"You could go to Pollensa on the north of the island," Maria suggested quickly. "They have wonderful beaches there."

"That's great," said Bill.

Laura put down her glass and stood up.

"Excuse me," she said and walked rigidly away toward the patio. Outside, she gulped in the cool late afternoon air with relief. Jared was doing his worst and she hated him for his cruelty. What was the matter with him? She was standing near the metal railing that ran around the patio to protect people from falling to the terrace twelve feet below when she heard someone come up behind her. She sensed it was Jared even before he spoke.

"I owe you an apology for my behavior this afternoon," Jared said quietly from beside her. "I've never been jealous before, so I didn't know what had gotten into me until just now."

Laura glanced up at him as he stood leaning forward against the railing looking down at the village. She folded her arms in front of her and gazed with him downward.

"Bill's a fine man," Jared went on softly. "He'll

make someone a good husband." He paused and Laura waited, knowing he would go on.

"But not for you," he concluded and he turned to look at her.

Laura raised her eyes to his, and when she saw the intensity of his look she felt a jolt.

"And why not for me?" she questioned in a low voice.

"Because a man can only be a good husband to a woman who loves him, and . . ." His eyes bore into hers . . . "you don't love him."

Even as she tried to look calmly back at him she could feel herself trembling.

"And what is that to you?" she whispered.

Jared stared at her a moment and then grimaced as if in pain.

"You're right, I suppose," he said. "I have no right to interfere."

"Then don't," Laura said and turned away to return to the living room. Bill was coming toward them.

"Laura, I thought you'd been out here a long time." He stopped and looked at Jared before going on: "I think you've both been rude. Please explain to me why you ran from the room?" Bill stood solidly in front of her, his hands in his pockets.

"Later, Bill, please," Laura pleaded.

"Why? And why are you out here with this fellow?"

"She's out here with this fellow," Jared announced, bringing himself up from his leaning position and standing squarely in front of Bill, "because this fellow followed her out here." Then he added unexpectedly, "I've got to go now, Bill. It's been good meeting you.

I hope you have a nice visit here. Good night Laura."
Nodding curtly in her direction, Jared wheeled and
strode rapidly off the patio around the side of the
house and began to descend to the village.

"What was that all about?" Bill demanded as he
watched him go.

"Where's Jared going?" Professor Johnson asked,
emerging out onto the patio with Eric.

"I don't know," said Bill. "He just took off."

"Well, good riddance," said Professor Johnson
tipsily. "That showboat writer never does what you
expect. Come on in. It's time for coffee and dessert."

"Laura?" said Bill, taking her arm as she still stood
watching the retreating figure of Jared. Slowly, like a
prisoner, Laura let herself be led back to the living
room.

Laura and Bill took their leave an hour later. Laura
felt strained to her limits with polite conversation.
When Dr. Johnson took her aside to ask her if she was
serious about leaving, she had to admit she hadn't
discussed it thoroughly with Bill.

"I don't know what's going on here, but I suggest
you get it straightened out soon, Laura."

"Yes, I will," Laura answered. "I'm sorry for the
confusion." Laura had been embarrassed at the awkward position in which Bill had placed her. The day
had been a disaster.

Laura and Bill walked back to the *pensión* in the
dusk. A soft wind rustled through the olive trees.
Laura hugged her wrap around herself.

"Are you cold?" Bill asked.

"No." She allowed Bill to take her elbow but held

herself stiffly. They walked on in silence until they reached the Villa Rojo.

"Are you angry with me about something, Laura?" Bill asked as he led her to a bench at the edge of the Villa's patio. The only light came from two square lit windows twenty feet away.

"Yes, I am," Laura answered. "You shouldn't have announced I was leaving here. You know I told you last night that I wasn't certain."

"I know, honey," Bill replied. "But at the Johnsons' *I* became certain. Our being apart hasn't been good for us. We seemed to be drifting apart. I think our arrangement has become too loose. It was a mistake."

"Bill, I want to talk to you about what's been happening here since . . ."

"Before you do, honey, I've got something important to say." Bill reached into his suit jacket pocket and brought something out, glanced at it and handed it to Laura.

"I want us to get married as soon as possible," Bill said, smiling proudly.

Slowly, reluctantly, Laura looked down at what Bill had placed in her hand. It was a small blue velvet box. Tensely she opened it. Even in the relative darkness of the patio the diamond sparkled.

"And since we'll be getting formally engaged, and then married in June," Bill went on, "there's no sense in your staying here, is there? We'll want to be together to plan the wedding."

Laura felt cold and lifeless. The ring meant nothing to her. Facing clearly at last the prospect of marrying Bill she realized fully and beyond doubt that she wasn't in love with him, didn't want to marry him. She closed the blue velvet box, still looking down at it.

"Do you like it?" Bill asked, reaching to hold her arms.

Laura raised her head to face him.

"Bill, listen to me a minute," she began, fearing he would again interrupt.

"I'm waiting, honey."

"Bill, I . . . can't marry you," she finally managed softly.

He stared at her in the dim light.

"What did you say?" he asked incredulously.

"I've always liked you, and I respect you. We've had fun. And I . . . I'll always think of you as a friend, a fine person, but . . . I can't marry you. I'm sorry."

"But *why!?*" Bill burst out in sudden anger. "I've just flown three thousand miles to be with you, just given you an expensive ring, and suddenly you're saying we're through!"

"I know it must seem sudden and unreasonable to you. It's hard to explain. I just know that I'm not ready to return; that I must finish my work here on Mallorca, and that . . . I've changed."

"Has it got something to do with Jared Tanner?" Bill snapped back at her.

"I don't know," she began hesitantly.

"You don't know!?" Bill exploded. "You're making a fool out of me and you don't *know?*"

Laura stood up, gently placing the ring in his hands. "I can't explain my feelings toward Jared," she said firmly. "But I do know that I can't marry you. You must understand."

"You're making a big mistake," Bill replied angrily, standing to confront her. "Throwing away a chance to marry me. You're right, I don't understand!"

"Bill, please, talking won't change how I feel. I . . . there's nothing more to say. I'll see you in the morning."

As she moved slowly away, Bill grabbed her by the arm and swung her around.

"I'm going to see Jared Tanner," he said, still flushed and more angry than she had ever seen him. "And get him to admit that he's been playing with you. Then maybe you'll come to your senses."

"No, Bill," she answered him firmly. "No matter what Jared says, it won't change anything. I'm sure in my own mind that I can't . . ."

"SHUT UP!" Bill shouted and, releasing her, hurried into the Villa.

Laura stood a moment in frozen silence and then slowly walked home. She had rejected a man who loved her for one who apparently didn't, but she knew it was the only thing to do. She loved Jared. Beyond that she didn't want to think.

Chapter Ten

The next two days were as depressing as Laura had ever experienced. Bill's flight back wasn't until Sunday noon so they had to endure forty-eight hours during which Bill at first tried to get her to change her mind and then spent his time sullenly implying she was a fool.

Although Jared seemed to have holed up in his house, Bill had managed to confront him there late the next day, but what took place Bill didn't make clear. He refused to talk about it. In any case he made no claim that Jared admitted he was "playing with her."

Sunday morning Bill had to leave. By mutual agreement she didn't accompany him down to the airport in Palma. They separated outside the taxi that was taking him down.

"You're making a big mistake, Laura," Bill said. "I don't know whether I'll be willing to give you a second chance."

"I'm sorry, Bill," Laura had replied, knowing she wasn't making a mistake in freeing herself of Bill. "I should have warned you before you flew over."

"I would have come anyway," he said. "Good-bye."

"Good-bye."

The parting had been that cold and was as dead as any love that had ever existed between them. When he was gone she felt mostly relief. There might be nothing between Jared and her but strong physical desire but at least she was free now to see if there was more.

But in Jared's class on Monday morning he was as cold and reserved as she had ever seen him, not even glancing at her. And when at one o'clock she reported to his apartment to resume her work with him there was only a brief note: "I'm working today. Report again tomorrow morning at ten."

The next day he let her in with great reserve, set her up with some work and disappeared upstairs. She heard him pacing back and forth for fifteen minutes and then he came stamping down the stairs.

"We're going for a drive," he announced abruptly.

"But why?" she said. "I thought you said you had some very important writing you had to do today."

"I do," he snapped back. "But I can't concentrate. I've got to get out of here. Let's go."

Laura suppressed a quick retort before she pulled on her sweater; doing battle with her tongue was a lot easier than doing battle with "the bear" before her. They walked to his car in silence. Laura had to admit she was happy to be with him even if she was apprehensive about his moodiness. He unlocked the car and opened the door for her.

"It's not such a good idea," she said. "You're in a rotten mood."

He got in and fired the engine.

"It will disappear soon." His profile had again that look of closed control. He was wearing his sheepskin vest and black cords, with a black sweater: his pirate look, she thought.

"You forgot your gaucho hat," she said, trying to lighten his mood as she slid in beside him. He manipulated the car into the highway, heading north along the coastline.

"It's not necessary," he said, his voice remote.

"Where are we going?" she asked, trying again to be conversational.

"To Pollensa. There's a beautiful beach there and some nice shops," he said. He pointed to the glove compartment. "Take a look at the map in there. It will give you a good idea of the route we're taking."

She did as he asked and found the village, and then she sat back, leaning her head against the head-rest.

"So what are your relations now with Bill?" he asked suddenly, not looking at her.

"There are none," she answered quietly. "I'm afraid we may not even be friends any longer."

The tires screeched as he took a curve too fast and she had to grab a handhold on the dashboard.

"I hope you didn't end it because of me," he said. "You know I'm not the marrying kind."

"I did it because I realized I've never really been in love with him," Laura replied. "Since you've promised me nothing, I expect nothing. Please slow down."

Jared now braked the car and slowed down.

"You have no reason to be angry with me," she added.

"I'm not angry," he snapped back. She saw his hands tighten slightly on the wheel.

"Yes, you are. If you're not coldly ordering me around, you're trampling on my feelings like a bull. And your so-called business manner borders on being plain bad manners."

He threw her a look. "I'd like to shake you until your teeth rattle," he challenged.

"Do it then, I'd rather have that!"

He pulled over to the side of the road, cut the engine and turned to her, his eyes angry, his body seeming to fill the car.

She stared at him, waiting, her eyes wide with expectation. She saw his chest rising and falling with the heat of his reaction until he slowly regained control.

"You're goading me," he said.

"No, I'm not! You've been impossible and you know it!"

He regarded her a moment, his eyes slowly emptying, his anger dissipating. He turned back to the wheel, putting his hands on it and sat looking out the window at the blue sky.

"I have to leave Mallorca for Los Angeles next month," he announced unexpectedly.

"What?"

"My agent has arranged a lucrative and challenging writing project, one I've been angling for for a year, and I'll have to leave." He was staring out the window at the chain of mountains receding off to their left.

"Is that what's upsetting you?" she asked, her throat constricted, making her voice sound higher than usual.

"Partly," he answered, still not looking at her. "It means that in three weeks I have to . . ." He turned to look at her, lines of tension creasing his face.

"You have to . . . what?" she asked softly.

"Decide what I'm going to do with my typist," he answered with sudden lightness.

"What would you like to do with her?" Laura asked.

Jared burst out laughing.

"I refuse to answer on the grounds of self-incrimination."

Laura found herself laughing too. "I'm glad," she said. "I hate it when you seem indifferent."

"I can never be indifferent to you, Laura," he said huskily and she felt that electrical connection between them again.

As Jared headed the car once again toward Pollensa, Laura tried to divert her attention to the scenery, making comments on what she saw and asking him about his past travels on the island. He answered in short sentences, again becoming frustratingly uncommunicative. Finally, they drove in silence, Laura staring out the window as the rugged scenery slid past. As they headed through a high mountain pass, deep gorges were visible along the road providing a splendid view.

"Can we stop and take a look?" she asked.

"If you like." He pulled over and sat quietly. After a moment he said, "Well? Aren't you getting out to look around?"

"Aren't you?" she asked him.

"No."

She boldly let her eyes rove on his face and over his body as he sat turned away from her, looking out the window, one browned hand resting on his thigh. She looked at it, remembering the time he pressed it against her at the Johnson's. His fingers curled.

"What are you waiting for, Laura?" he asked.

"You," she answered spontaneously. "I love you."

His hand clenched on his thigh. He slowly turned, his face mirroring an anguish she hadn't known he was capable of. His eyes examined hers, diving into them as if he could see into her soul. Letting out a breath, he let his head fall back against the seat.

"I must be losing my mind," he said, giving a low, tight laugh. His hand moved, the palm opening on his thigh. "What do you want me to do?" he asked.

"I . . . nothing," Laura's voice failed as she let out her breath. "I want to end the war of nerves between us. I'm sorry if I said the wrong thing."

He turned away.

"You've taken it back already," he said flatly.

"No."

He jerked his body up and turned the engine on, pulling out into the highway again.

"You think love is something in a book, a fairy tale," he charged. "You thought you loved Bill and now you think you love me. Hardly a realiable emotion in your case. I don't think you know what you want." Jared's eyes were glued on the road as he drove. Laura folded her hands in front of her.

"I only know I love you, nothing more," she said in a firm voice. "I want to be with you, to see you. I was in such pain when you were in London with May. The moment I saw Bill again I realized I wasn't in love with him. I know you think I'm some kind of unformed idiot where emotions are concerned, but I know how I feel."

"Laura . . ." he began in a husky voice. "If I took you at your word, I wouldn't turn back. I couldn't, make no mistake about it." He looked over at her a moment, his lips compressed. "I wouldn't stand for your playing with me, or turning back either. I'd make life miserable for both of us. It may be more than you bargained for. I won't play at love, Laura; you'd be mine, chauvinist pig that I am." His lips curled in a sardonic smile. "You'd have to accept it, and me, as I am."

"And May?" she whispered back, stunned by his unexpected words, her heart beating faster.

He was silent a moment.

"May," he said without intonation, pausing. "I never was in love with May. Do you want to hear about her?" He glanced over at her.

She said nothing. Her heart was in her throat as she tried to follow him.

"We had an affair in New York. I met her at a party and took her back to my apartment. No questions asked, no games, just sex. That's how I thought about it. When I left New York, I never expected to see her again. As far as I was concerned, it was over. I had no idea she would follow me here, and none that she wanted more. That's a male pig, I guess, in your eyes. She expected to pick up where we left off and add something permanent. Marriage. But I've never been the marrying kind and May was never that special to me. We said all we had to say before she went to London. I didn't sleep with her here, Laura. I didn't want to." He gave her a quick look. "My guess is she's quite happy now in London. May is ambitious. She wants more than modeling and doing TV commercials. She met a man in London that can help her get the acting parts she wants. I saw much less of her here than it may have appeared to you. I felt some guilt and didn't want to cut her any more than I had to. Can you understand that?"

He finished and, as if he had gotten a great load off his chest, he seemed easier. His face lost some of its controlled hardness.

"No reactions?" he said finally, glancing at her.

Laura was twisted sideways on the seat to face him, her head resting on the seat, her eyes on him. Her hands were tense; her breathing was less than easy.

"You're honest," she said.

"With you, yes."

"I think you've been with everyone."

"Would you call my treatment of May honest?" he asked.

"Yes. It may not be romantic, but it's honest."

"Thank you." A bare smile slanted on his lips.

"It doesn't change anything," she said, stretching her denim-clad legs out.

She saw his hands relax on the wheel.

"You still want to start your love life with me?"

No, she thought, *I want to end it with you.* But there was still the barrier of his not committing himself. He had never said he loved her and until she understood better his deepest feelings—or he understood them—

they could never come fully together. She didn't quite see a way around this yet, but she felt that a way would present itself.

"Yes," she answered him, even as her logic was shouting no.

He took in his breath and looked at her, a brilliant light in his eyes, and then he clamped down on it. He was silent a few moments.

"No. I can't and won't let it happen," he said at last, his voice low. His face was relaxed, as if the decision was so final in his mind that it was unshakable.

"You're going to withdraw again?" she said. "That's not fair to me."

"It's very fair," his hand reached over, almost touching her before he caught himself and drew it back.

"Afraid?" she taunted him, wishing that he had touched her.

"You're trying to tease me, playing a game you can only get hurt at. Fortunately for you, I've been there and I know it when I see it. Now behave yourself."

They arrived at the beautiful little village of Pollensa. White, yellow, and pink houses ringed a horseshoe-shaped sandy beach. A huge, wide bay stretched before them, ringed by mountains except for a narrow passage out to sea. Jared drove slowly along the beachfront road until he found a parking place.

"Like it?" he asked her, smiling, referring to the view.

"It's very pretty." Laura's mind returned to the more important subject to her. "I feel you're still not sharing with me all of your feelings."

"I'm not," he said, taking the keys out of the ignition. "Because I don't believe in sharing feelings I'm still not certain of." He opened his car door. "Let's go eat lunch. I know you well enough to know you have a healthy appetite." He got out of the car.

Laura was beginning to feel defeated. She hated his holding back from her. He opened her door and stood back, holding it wide, and then locked it behind her.

"Let's buy some bread and cheese and eat on the beach," she asked. "I don't feel like being in a restaurant just now."

She could feel the wind playing lightly with her hair. Two boats were anchored in the wide bay and the beach was almost deserted. The tourist season was not in full swing now, although a few camera-toting characters strolled leisurely around the shops and sat in the outdoor cafés along the sidewalk. The residents were at work and the children in school. It was unspoiled and quiet. They went into a little store and bought a simple supply of food with wine and oranges as treats. Laura picked out a small packet of cookies and Jared bought a soft straw basket to put everything in and slipped its narrow rope handles over his shoulder.

He was smiling in a pleasant easy way. He was patiently amused at her enjoyment of the village craft shops and followed her in while she browsed enthusiastically, exclaiming over the variety of talents displayed. While she was examining all the olive-wood chess sets, sculptures, and a variety of bowls, beads, and articles beautifully carved and polished, he bought her a black silk shawl she had admired, with a long fringe and embroided red red roses in its center.

When she caught him paying for the shawl, she was disturbed by his purchase and told him so.

He reminded her, smiling, about his feelings regarding his money. "Gifts are reminders of our mutual dependence on one another, our need for each other. It's more than being ungracious to refuse, it's an insult. We're friends! If you cooked a meal for me and I refused to eat it, not because I wasn't hungry, but for some obscure idea that it was wrong of you to do that, wouldn't you be hurt or insulted? Think of it as an opportunity to let someone else express his feelings. That way you're giving a gift back for the one received."

"Help! I'm in love with Socrates." She arched an eyebrow at him. He had dispelled her embarrassment by his lecture, and her reaction was spontaneous, but she also saw that she was returning his gift with her expression of how she felt, straight from the heart. He would have to eat his words. She grinned at him.

He looked down at her, a light gleaming in his eyes. "I wonder if they make olive-wood paddles. It's a very enduring hardwood, I've been told. Shall we inquire?" he asked.

She laughed at the hint.

They strolled down to the waterfront, Jared leaving her for a minute to put the shawl in the car. Laura sat down on the sand to remove her shoes, but after putting her feet in the cold water she retreated quickly to warm them in the sun-heated sand.

Jared sat leaning against a rock and, opening the basket, began putting together simple sandwiches, as he had done up on the mountain. He uncorked the wine and poured some in paper cups. Watching his slow, sure movements, she felt a surge of love for him.

"You're a very sweet man," she said with feeling.

He handed her a cup, looking directly at her. His sensuous mouth curled faintly in a smile, "And you're very lovely, and now that we've paid our compliments, eat." His voice as he spoke the last word was almost rough. She moved to sit next to him against the rock and ate quietly. When she had finished with her sandwich, she began to peel an orange and broke off a section, offering it to him. He raised his hand to take it from her.

"No. Open," she said, bringing it up to his lips. He slanted her a look and took it from her fingers and ate it, silently refusing her gesture.

"Oh, stubborn, thou art. And also unable to live up to your own teachings. I may not have cooked that orange, but you certainly refused to take it from me! I'm insulted," she said teasingly.

He said nothing to refute her and leaned back, closing his eyes, the sun on his face.

"Why don't you take off your shoes and put your feet in the sand? It feels great," she said.

He stretched his legs out. "I'm going to take a *siesta*. Leave me in peace, woman, I've been through enough today." He relaxed, his arms down on the sand.

Laura straightened up, getting to her feet. "You're right, you're too sophisticated for me. You have no play left in you. You're all cold dignity and stiff control." She kicked some sand at his feet and marched off. She had said it all mockingly, but she hoped it would upset him a little. She was put off by his refusal of her and yet his acceptance of her presence.

She walked along the beach and, seeing a toy stand, she bought a beach ball. Slowly walking back to Jared, she called to him as he lay on his back in the sand, his sheepskin vest making a pillow.

"Catch!" she called, and threw it at him, hoping it would reach where she intended it. She tossed it in a high arc, but it headed right for him. He reached out and caught it. She stood with her hands on her hips. "If you're too decrepit to get on your feet, you can toss it to me from there."

He sat up, grinning.

"You're talking to a soccer champ," he said, throwing the ball at her.

She skipped aside and chased after it, kicking it once away from him, then turning and dribbling it through the sand with her bare feet. He had gotten to his feet and they kicked it back and forth. Jared began using his knees and head and Laura followed his lead until the ball bounced into the water.

"Oh, no!" She watched the ball floating away. "Well, at least I got you to work off some of that writer's fat," she said, walking over to him, waiting for his reaction.

He smiled and held out his hand. "Come on, let's go for a walk in town." It was the first time he had touched her all day. It was unbearably sweet. Her hand closed around his possessively, not wanting ever to let it go. She drew herself closer to his side. He had robbed her of her playful moment, but riddled her with fierce pleasure.

He released her hand with a quick movement and moved away from her. She gave him a questioning look.

"Go get your shoes," he said, running his hand through his hair in agitation. She left him abruptly and sat in the sand pulling on her shoes.

He could thrust her away so easily. He might not admit it, but the feeling between them was too strong to dismiss; it was no gently falling snow on a mild day, but a blizzard.

Jared was waiting for her on the sidewalk looking idly at some postcards outside and making polite conversation with the proprietress of the shop. Laura approached him shyly as he turned and ran his eyes briefly over her in a look that was almost a caress. Jared put his hand on the curve of her waist to guide her along the sidewalk. The warmth of his hand threw her into confusion, especially as he had just refused her touch.

"I hope I'll be able to speak Spanish as easily as you one day," Laura said, striving for a calm conversation amid the warm joy of her feelings.

He guided her into a tourist shop with handsome displays of all kinds of arts and crafts. Laura was determined not to admire anything in a way that he could interpret as desire for the object. He picked up the conversation.

"I grew up with some Spanish in my home," he said, stopping in front of a display of jewelry.

"You're Spanish?" she asked him, suddenly putting together both his fluency and his dark coloring.

"No, but I had a Spanish grandmother who lived with us. I learned to speak English and Spanish simultaneously." He spoke with a salesgirl and asked to see several pairs of earrings, looking at them carefully and holding them up to Laura's ear. The light touch of his fingertips against her face moved her deeply.

"Jared . . ." she began softly, wanting to protest, but a glance from him told her to hold it in. He bought two pairs of unusually beautiful earrings, large gold filigree loops and a pair of long silver ones with a green semiprecious stone at the tip. As they left the store Jared gave her the little package. Again his simple gesture touched her to the point of pain.

"If you don't want me to care for you, don't give me gifts, please," she said.

"I never said I didn't want you to care for me," he said quietly, guiding her again with his hand at her waist. "Want to go someplace else? We can drive along the coast and then cut back home."

"Yes," she answered distractedly, and then added: "Do you want me to love you? Why do you give me presents with one hand, but hold me away from you with the other. I don't understand what you're doing."

"Then don't worry about it. Maybe there's not much to understand. Perhaps I care for you enough not to take my pleasure and run. You aren't May. I feel differently about you. I have no desire to acquire a guilty conscience. It doesn't mean I don't enjoy being with you or want you any less. It's possible you're ready for a lover—in fact, you are—but there's much more to it than that for me with you."

Laura turned away from him, looking blindly ahead. She sensed love in his words but he had again avoided committing himself. Getting into the car she avoided looking at him and leaned her head back on the seat and closed her eyes. He took a road along the coast into the setting sun. A long silence followed.

"Laura, I'm sorry," he finally said. "I don't mean to hurt or confuse you. Don't you want to have a few years of independence? I thought that's what you wanted."

"Why should you care?" she whispered huskily.

"I do care."

"Kind of you," she said.

"I guess we'd better drop the subject," he said abruptly and drove on in silence. Ten minutes later they drew up outside a restaurant on the beach nestled among a string of hotels and night spots. It was dark now and the beams of the moon made a silver path down the sea toward them.

Laura decided she would not make their dinner something they would both regret. Jared seemed to feel the same. After asking her what she wanted, he ordered *gazpacho* and *paella* and two whiskey sours. Then he asked her about her life at home and why she had written plays before stories and who her favorite writers were. Laura's answers were subdued. She was aware of it and began to try for lightness but only succeeded in a soft reticence.

She was depressed by his ambivalence and beyond caring if her mood showed. After they'd talked about her, Jared told her several amusing anecdotes about his career. Gradually she began to loosen up, smiling at the comic scenes he described. Once he'd gone to be interviewed along with another author only to discover a mix-up had produced as his co-interviewee a famous horse trainer. "Neither of us knew anything about the other's work, but by the time they finished editing the tape it appeared we were friends of centuries and that horse training and novel writing were closely related arts."

Laura began to feel that now they could talk about anything. She no longer felt any of her earlier inhibitions. Even as he seemed to be rejecting an intimate relationship she could see that he accepted her as a person.

At the end of their meal Jared reached over and took her hand and their conversation stopped as if by mutual agreement. As they looked into each other's eyes their feelings flowed without check. Laura knew in that moment that he loved her. That he wouldn't yet verbalize it; that something was still holding him back. The one thing she couldn't bear to think about was the day they would have to part. So little time! She wanted to live with him, to share his joys and cares, but it wasn't to be. She only barely managed to hold back her tears. Finally, he smiled tenderly, squeezing her hand before relinquishing it, and called for the check.

Laura was drowsy on the way back. She fell into a light sleep, her head resting against his shoulder. A contentment mixed with desire blended in their being together. When he drew up outside her *pensión* he put his hand on her knee.

"Laura, are you awake?"

She awoke, instantly aware of him.

"Very," she said, smiling up at him.

"Come as early as you can tomorrow."

"How early?"

"As soon as you're free."

Impulsively she leaned over to brush his lips gently with hers. He took in his breath and stopped her with a strong grip on her arms.

"Why not?" she asked tremulously. "Just once."

He relaxed his arms and ran a hand under her chin, bending slowly to brush his lips against hers. It was like lighting dry grass with a careless match. Laura leaned into him bringing her arms around his neck, one hand in his hair. He made a low sound in his throat as he took possession of her mouth. He lifted her into his arms, pressing her against him tightly. Laura greedily gave and took his caresses and his deep kisses. They were making up for the weeks they hadn't rushed into each other's arms. When Jared pulled away from her lips he put his hand on her throat, his warm breath fanning her face.

"That's why not," he whispered hoarsely. "I want no regrets with you. I don't want your disgust or your disappointment, if I can help it." He slid his hand softly down her body, gently caressing her breast on the way down to her waist.

"Jared, take me back with you."

He let out a breath and stopped his lazy teasing kisses and moved her out of his arms.

"Out you go." His voice assumed a firmer sound. "As it is, you've stirred the fire too much and you know it. Go on," he leaned over, giving her a gentle shove, and opened the door.

"I don't understand you," she said.

"Not yet, but you will."

"What happened to the pirate?"

He laughed softly.

"No one would believe the irony of this situation: You trying to seduce me and I, reluctant pirate, desperately holding out." His eyes checked their light. "Good night, Laura."

"Good night," she said, and left him, listening in the dark for the sound of his car until it faded.

Chapter Eleven

The next day Laura felt a suppressed excitement, a joy that centered on the presence of Jared or the thought of his soon appearing. There was a lightness to her movements and a feeling of warmth toward everyone and everything around her. In the rare moment that she allowed herself to remember that he had never said "I love you" or committed himself to her in words that she understood, she had doubts, and quickly tried her best to forget them. She admitted to herself that he could be just playing with her and knew that if this was true, she would be annihilated. Then she would immediately think of the loving things he had said, knowing that she had only her intuition to rely on. For her, there was no turning back. If she was about to be burned, the butterfly would have to exist without wings or perish. Her love was irrevocable. It had no boundaries. She would fly to her mate and she hoped the mate she chose would want her by his side.

Laura pulled on a royal-blue sweater and changed into a simple black skirt and wool knee-socks. Her room, in fact all the stone buildings, while cool in summer, were cold in fall and winter. It was only near a fire or in a small heated room that one could get warm without a lot of clothing. Jared, however, always had a fire for her and she worked in a cozy corner right next to it.

When she arrived to do more typing, he was dressed for town in a black sweater under a light-brown sports jacket and dark gray pants. He looked wonderful.

"Handsome," was all she could say. "I don't know whether you really are or it's just me who thinks so." She slipped her arms around him. He held her for a moment, but she could sense the restraint he had placed on himself, a burying of his instincts. It frustrated her.

"Don't withdraw from me," she said. "It's so heavenly when you let down your guard. Please." She smiled at him, capturing his eyes.

"You'd seduce a saint," he muttered, before he bent his warm lips to hers. His hands pressed her hips to him. She felt a shudder go through him as he withdrew. Laura's eyes drowned in his. He took her arms to hold her away from him.

"You keep pushing and testing me." He hesitated a moment; his dark eyes going serious. "Laura . . ." he seemed to be debating whether to say something and then seemed to decide against it. He sighed.

"I'm going to Palma on business," he said. "Don't wait for me to return, I'll be back late. Everything's organized. Throw a log on the fire when it gets low."

"Do you have to go?" she asked. "Is it to avoid being with me?"

He turned a shoulder in her direction.

"That too," he said, smiling at her.

Laura searched his face, struggling with her wish to keep him with her.

"You realize we've only a week left to be together," he said softly, as if he understood her reluctance to let them part and felt it himself. She didn't try to hide the distress his words gave her and was unable to answer him.

"I can't stay," he said, as much to himself as to her. As he put his hand on the door to open it he added:

"Would you consider studying writing someplace else?"

Laura was feeling too lost at the thought of their separation to consider why he asked. "It would be foolish not to, I suppose," she answered without thinking.

He looked hard at her a moment. "We'll talk about it again. Come here," he said on a softer note, reaching out an arm to encircle her. When she came without hesitation into the circle of his arms, he pressed her to him, brushing his warm lips against hers tenderly.

"I don't want to leave you," he whispered. His hand tightened on her waist. "But if I don't go, you might not get the typing finished, or even started, not with the way I feel about you today." He took her lips in a brief, longing kiss, and then released her. "Get to work, or I'll never get this book done. And don't wait for me; I'll be late." He gave her a smile and a playful shove toward the typewriter. Opening the door, he left without looking back.

Like a husband going off to work, thought Laura, as

she put a hand to her lips as if to touch their kiss. Slowly she recovered her senses and started to type, but it was awhile before she really got to work.

She worked late, taking breaks to feed the fire and herself. It felt good to roam around Jared's house freely. She went up to his bedroom, feeling a leaping of her heart to see his neatly made bed, a table scattered with his papers where he worked while she typed. His jeans, carelessly draped over a chair with a sweater and T-shirt, exuded his presence, and she touched them lightly with her hand. Finally she turned to go back and finish the typing.

Hoping he might come home earlier than he had said, she dragged out her stay. Finally, she came to the end of the section he had planned for her. On the bottom of the last page, in his script, were the words, "Until tomorrow, know that I love you, Jared."

Laura sat staring at the words. Getting up from the chair, she walked in a daze around the room, her heart filled with a joy she hadn't believed possible. She went back to the paper to read it again, to be sure she hadn't dreamed them. They weren't a part of the text. It was a message for her. All that was left was to hear the words from his own lips. They were all the encouragement she needed for her confidence to soar. She had no intention of going home without seeing him.

Building up the fire, washing up the dishes, and tidying, she waited. Finally, tired, she took herself upstairs and walked into his room, looking down at his bed. Her pulse quickened and she trembled slightly as she decided what she was going to do. She longed to be with him in the fullest sense, wanted to have his arms around her, his lips on hers; needed his words of love, his caresses. Slowly undressing, all her doubts gone, she slipped between the sheets. For a long time she lay awake, listening for the sound of his car, his entrance through the door. She was in turn restless with anticipation and fatigued from her own excitement. She drifted off to sleep with warm thoughts of lying in Jared's arms.

She felt, rather than heard him. She was suddenly awake, aware in the dark of Jared sitting on the edge of the bed. When she made a slight sound with her accelerated breathing, she felt him respond. He reached over with one hand and in the darkness found her face and lightly caressed it.

"Laura," he said softly, but when she reached for him he rose off the bed and turned on the light, staring down at her, his hands on his hips.

"I should have known," he said in a low voice. She could see him take in a deep breath as he saw her bare shoulders.

He came back to the bed again and put his arms on either side of her body, tightening the blankets and imprisoning her. She wriggled one arm free and reached out to put her warm hand on his arm. The touch of his skin sent warmth flooding through her. She couldn't speak, letting her eyes and softly parted lips say what her tongue would not. His brown eyes locked with hers, intensely alert, and then softened as they roved over her throat, her bare shoulders. As she ran her hand caressingly over his arm she felt his muscles tense beneath her touch.

"Are you sure you know what you're doing?" he asked huskily. Laura saw his eyes were liquid with love.

"I only know I love you," she said softly.

It seemed to sober him to hear her speak. His face showed a checking, a slight withdrawal. He hesitated as he bent to her. He took her by the shoulders, his hands tightening on her bare arms, and then gathered her up into his arms. His hand on her naked back sent shivers of pleasure through her. Feeling her tremors, he withdrew his hand and looked into her eyes.

"You have me almost crazy with wanting you," he whispered, but reluctantly let her go, drawing the blankets up to cover her completely.

"I want you to make love to me," she whispered, reaching for him. "I want to be your woman, at least once."

"So, you got my note," he said softly.

"Yes."

"And you decided to wait for me." A smile curved his lips.

She nodded.

"And then what?"

"Whatever you want." She said it softly, with the artless unrehearsed perfection of a woman in love.

"No thought for consequences?" He uncoiled his body and sat again on the bed near her.

"I love you and I trust you," she replied simply.

He drew her gently into his arms, holding the blankets around her body. He touched his lips briefly to hers.

"And I love you," he said.

The words were uttered with an intensity that took her breath away and quickened her whole being.

"It's beyond anything I imagined," he went on in a low voice. "There were times when I ached for you—so much . . . especially when I felt your willingness to surrender yourself to me. That gift, the most precious thing in the world to me, I could only accept when I was sure . . . That's why I've wanted to go slow, to hold myself back." Now he framed her face with his hands, gently caressing it, and his eyes were pouring love into hers.

"I've had the other kind of love," he went on, "and I knew I wanted something deeper with you." He kissed her at last, but so soaring was she from his words that the transition from words to lips was barely perceptible. Only when he finally broke gently away did she fully realize that their mouths had been melting in a kiss.

"But now that I'm certain I love you, it's still important that you be certain too," he went on. "I want you to be able to give yourself to me without reservations, without regret. I want you to be sure. I don't want you to wake up one day and discover that I kept you from something more important. We can grow together. I know I can let you do that freely, but I want your commitment."

"But you have it, Jared," she cried in response. "You have it." Then she laughed. "Are you purposefully frustrating me?"

He laughed.

"A little, yes. You can't imagine what I feel, can you?" He kissed her temple and brushed her cheeks with his lips. "I want nothing more in the world than to take what you're offering me. I want you to know that I'm playing for a lifetime."

Laura felt dizzy from his words and radiant smile. "I don't know what I'm doing anymore. I'll do anything you ask. I'm so in love with you." Laura ran her fingers lovingly along his neck and shoulders. He was still slightly cold from being in the November air.

"Jared," she began softly, uncertainly. "Are we still going to have to part in December?"

He looked at her with a teasing smile.

"That all depends," he replied.

"Depends on what?" she asked.

"Do you think you could be happy in Los Angeles?" he asked softly. "They have a good graduate writing program there."

"With you?"

"Do you have someone else in mind?"

Laura swallowed. It was what she wanted although not a perfect ending since he still hadn't . . .

"As my wife?" he whispered against her ear.

Her head came up to look into his face, to make certain of what she had heard. His eyes were filled with light. A cry of joy came softly out of her, and then, eyes sparkling, she answered, "I'll think about it."

He looked at her with laughing eyes.

"The way things are going I think we'd better marry here and right away, if that's all right with you."

She simply stared at him in bliss, parting her lips and searching for his.

"I told you," she whispered, "anything you want."

"Shameless woman," he whispered against her

mouth. His arms tightening around her, pressing her along his body. "If my book fails it's because around you I couldn't think straight."

"Our lives together will be the best story we'll ever write," she whispered back and would have said more but her lips were now commanded by his.

Coming Next Month

Song of Surrender by Elizabeth Hunter

A temperamental and exacting taskmaster, David Lloyd wanted Katy as his pupil. Katy knew this would advance her singing career, but could she resist the sweet insistence of his lovemaking?

Less of A Stranger by Nora Roberts

Megan and David clashed over his plans for the amusement park she ran. But Megan wanted the restless, roaming David, and at Joyland, dreams were supposed to come true.

The Felstead Collection by Kay Stephens

Jay was hired to determine whether the paintings in the priceless Felstead collection were real. But soon she was wondering if the love of dark, enigmatic Rhys Felstead was a true one.

Silhouette Romance

Coming Next Month

Roomful of Roses by Diana Palmer

Only one thing stood in the way of Wynn's marriage—her legal guardian, McCabe Foxe. The tough war correspondent invaded her life again—and lay siege to her heart.

Best of Enemies by Joan Smith

Toni Ewell and Jack Beldon drew battle lines over the planned demolition of a town landmark. But sometimes the best of enemies can turn into something more than friends.

No Gentle Love by Ruth Langan

It took a man like Drew Carlson to recognize the sensuality beneath Kate Halloran's tailored suit. He hoped she'd find a love that wasn't forecast in the annual reports.

Silhouette Romance

95p each

280 ☐ SULLIVAN'S WOMAN
Nora Roberts

281 ☐ A TENDER PASSION
Thea Lovan

282 ☐ IF EVER I LOVED YOU
Phyllis Halldorson

283 ☐ STIRRINGS OF THE HEART
Tiffany Payne

284 ☐ IRRESISTIBLE INTRUDER
Karen Young

285 ☐ THE GENTLING
Ginna Gray

286 ☐ THE MAN FROM THE PAST
Dorothy Cork

287 ☐ PERMANENT FIXTURE
Janet Joyce

288 ☐ CHANCE OF A LIFETIME
Joan Smith

289 ☐ PARTNERS IN LOVE
Jean Saunders

290 ☐ RAIN ON THE WIND
Elizabeth Hunter

291 ☐ THE SINGING STONE
Rena McKay

292 ☐ PAYMENT IN FULL
Anne Hampson

293 ☐ BEHIND CLOSED DOORS
Diana Morgan

294 ☐ BELOVED PIRATE
Ann Cockcroft

295 ☐ THAT TENDER FEELING
Dorothy Vernon

296 ☐ SOUTH OF THE SUN
Laurie Paige

297 ☐ A SEPARATE HAPPINESS
Brittany Young

All these books are available at your local bookshop or newsagent, or can be ordered direct from the publisher. Just tick the titles you want and fill in the form below.

Prices and availability subject to change without notice.

SILHOUETTE BOOKS, P.O. Box 11, Falmouth, Cornwall.

Please send cheque or postal order, and allow the following for postage and packing:

U.K. – 55p for one book, plus 22p for the second book, and 14p for each additional book ordered up to a £1.75 maximum.

B.F.P.O. and EIRE – 55p for the first book, plus 22p for the second book, and 14p per copy for the next 7 books, 8p per book thereafter.

OTHER OVERSEAS CUSTOMERS – £1.00 for the first book, plus 25p per copy for each additional book.

Name ....

Address ....

....